WHY YOU SHOULD READ THIS BOOK

Because it answers questions and needs that no other book does!

Today there are many very good "sex manuals" to clear up the mysteries of the physiology of sex, the mechanics of sensual pleasure and variety, and even good books and courses on the psychology of sex. In addition, we are currently experiencing a re-birth in belief in romance, and there is genuine recognition of the need for better communication between lovers and marriage partners.

There are even many good books from the Eastern Tradition explaining the involvement of the subtle energies and psychic centres in sexual relations.

But — until now there has been no book on the true *Magick of Sex*. Yet the Western Tradition is even richer than the books on the Tantra and the Tao of Sex in awareness of the inner dimensions of Love and Sex. And the Western Tradition is rich in knowledge of the techniques for adding Romance to the relationship, even to an older relationship where "young love" may seem to have died. And *the Magick of Sex* is rich in techniques for re-awakening and stimulating the natural psychological, and psychic, growth processes that for most people stop at adulthood and that should be ongoing as a part of every mature relationship.

Beyond these important steps to the establishment of the real, "inner" meaning of the "marriage of two souls," there is their attainment of the spiritual dimension and the reciprocal building of Magical and Spiritual Power. Here, in the ultimate achievement of their partnership, Man and Woman become One in the bringing of Success and Abundance to their material lives, and then — if they choose — *to consciously reach to the highest dimensions of their spirituality to bring about the conception of a child fully incarnating their love, their ideals, and the Blessing of the Divine Power.*

About the Authors

Melita Denning and Osborne Phillips, the authors of this book, are internationally recognized authorities on occultism, the Western Mystery Traditions, the psychology of the religious experience.

They are listed in a number of reference works, including *Who's Who in the World* and the *Dictionary of International Biography.* Their profound researches into the religious mysteries and magical practices, and their many years of intense practical involvement in Initiate Orders amply qualify them to make this knowledge available to the average person.

To Write to the Authors:

We encourage readers to write to the authors about their progress in applying the methods described in this book. We cannot guarantee that every letter will receive reply, but the authors will appreciate hearing of your success, and occasionally may be able to answer questions. We would also be happy to notify readers who request it, should the authors be making an appearance in their locality. Write to Melita Denning and Osborne Phillips
     c/o Llewellyn Publications
     P.O. Box 43383-MS, St. Paul, MN 55164-0383, U.S.A.

About The Llewellyn Practical Guides
to Personal Power

PRACTICAL: available, usable, and valuable in actions applied
to useful purposes, contributing toward a better
life.

That's what we mean when we say these books are "practical."
The knowledge is communicated in a manner that makes it immediately available and usable to the reader: it's not speculative
or abstract knowledge, nor merely informative or entertaining.

And it is valuable! Here are techniques that will help you to a
better life, will help you attain things that you want, will help
you in your personal growth and development. More than that,
these books can change your life, dynamically, positively.

Success aginst all obstacles! Miracles of healing! Powers
of ESP, psycho-kinesis, out-of-body travel! Clairvoyance
and divination of the future! Amazing powers of mind and
body! Attainment of all desires! Communication with non-
physical beings! Knowledge by non-material means!

We've always known of things like this . . . seemingly supernormal
achievements, often by quite ordinary people. Are these things
really possible? Can such powers be ours? Can we actually take
control of our own lives?

Yes, we know that many things are possible, and yet we so rarely
achieve all that we desire. We are told that we use only 10% of
our mental capacity, that faith can move mountains, that love
heals all hurt. We believe, but we lack practical knowledge.

All things that you will ever want must have their start in your
mind. In these books you are given practical knowledge and
progressive exercises to develop your inner powers. You are given
specific techniques for the application of these powers. These
abilities will eventually belong to everybody through natural
evolution: you can attain them now through self-directed
programs of development and training.

OTHER BOOKS FROM THE AUTHORS

The Magical Philosophy, Books 1 through 5
Book I, Robe and Ring, 1974
Book II, The Apparel of High Magick, 1975
Book III, The Sword and the Serpent, 1975
Book IV, The Triumph of Light, 1978
Book V, Mysteria Magica, 1982

The Llewellyn Practical Guide to Astral Projection, 1979
The Llewellyn Practical Guide to Creative Visualization, 1980
The Llewellyn Practical Guide to Psychic Self-Defense
and Well-Being, 1980
The Llewellyn Practical Guide to Development
of Psychic Powers, 1981
The Llewellyn Practical Guide to the Magick of Sex, 1982

Voudoun Fire: The Living Reality of Mystical Religion, 1979

The Llewellyn Deep Mind Tape for Astral Projection, 1981

Other Books Forthcoming in the Practical Guide series during 1982
The Llewellyn Practical Guide to Planetary Magick
The Llewellyn Practical Guide to Evocation of the Gods

Write for full list of forthcoming titles
and current information on related publications.
Llewellyn Publications
P.O. Box 43383-MS, St. Paul, MN 55164-0383, U.S.A.

The Llewellyn Practical Guide to

The Magick
of Sex

by Melita Denning and Osborne Phillips

1982
Llewellyn Publications
St. Paul, Minnesota, 55164-0383, U.S.A.

International Standard Book Number: 0-87542-191-1
First Edition 1982
First Printing 1982

Production by Llewellyn Publications
Publication by Llewellyn Publications
Typography & Art property of Chester-Kent, Inc.

LLEWELLYN PUBLICATIONS
A Division of Chester-Kent, Inc.
P.O. Box 43383
St. Paul, MN 55164-0383, U.S.A.

Printed in the United States of America

Illustrations by Joanne Westbrook

Cover Art by Roger Boehm

Introduction

STAR FIRE AND THE MAGICK OF SEX

There's a power and glory in sex that — even in these days of enlightenment and liberation — is generally not perceived. We sometimes experience momentary exaltations from these other dimensions of sex, but to perceive them we have to change our attitude about sex — even about life — itself.

In this "New Age" we are learning new attitudes and seeing more things from a "wholistic" perspective — but that itself is less new than we might suppose: it's just been long forgotten and buried beneath the weight of "partistic" data coming from the developing physical and psychological sciences.

Even now the "wholistic movement" is far less whole than is the far older "magical" way of seeing things. Modern thinking has indeed discovered that the Whole *can* be greater than its parts — but we are still looking at many "wholes" rather than making the great leap in our way of relating to the world-at-large to perceive the total unity of which every smaller "whole" (or entity or system) is an *integral* part.

Wholistic Medicine, for example, accepts the idea that we must look at the *whole* person in assessing health and treating disease, but "Magical Medicine" looks beyond the whole person to his inter-connections with the greater whole of the World in which we live — *visible and invisible!*

So it is with Sex. "Wholistic Sex," we might say, will go beyond the pure physiology and mechanics of sex to include psychological and cultural understanding, and might perhaps even include the subtle energy centres and systems recognized in the Tantra and the Tao of Sex. But *The Magick of Sex* goes yet further: seeing these psychic centres and subtle energy systems as connections to far vaster dimensions of Spirit and the Universe, and showing how we may bring these greater dimensions into our personal fields of awareness and application.

Yes, we say that it is Sex that gives life to the body, and that Sex is the dynamic that colors every aspect of culture, religion and society — but also we see Sex as the polarized energy that manifests and moves the World and that sets the Stars on Fire!

And, just as we have learned to control "fire" to cook our foods, warm our bodies and fuel our industry, so may we learn to work with Sex at all the different levels of relatedness in the body, the psyche, and the

Spirit of the person — and of that person's relatedness to his or her partner, and of that couple's relatedness to the many levels and planes of existence in the Universe — *visible and invisible* — as a whole.

The Magick of Sex teaches us how to enrich our lives and our sexual relationship, to tap the energies of body and psyche both for greater health and well-being and for a finer sex-life, and to expand our consciousness and contact the higher energies and forms of existence to make a better material life and a richer spiritual life.

And, it teaches us that we can consciously reach to the very heights of our spirituality in the conception of a child!

In Tantra we are told of the tremendous power that lies in the 'base' centre of body and psyche, called the *Serpent Fire*. And in Tantric Yoga we learn that through the arousing and directing of this great Serpent Fire we can attain other levels of consciousness and various psychic powers.

But there is another great power that we can contact in the Magick of Sex: the *Star Fire* that is the pure white flame of Divinity within each of us. And it is love that is the key here, for what one loves is the essential goodness, the Divinity, that we see in our beloved. That which we love is our partner's Higher Self, a true fragment of the Divine Mind. *When your attention is focussed upon the Higher Self, you are making love to a sacred person, Divine Person, Body, Soul and Spirit.*

"Making Love" then becomes a true form of *worship,* and it is *mutual* worship of the Divine Spark in each partner that opens the way for the full Power and Glory of the Star Fire to fill your being!

Our authors write:

To see Divinity in, and through, the beloved is to experience Divinity as love: a personal inward realization which can but overflow to transform the experiencer's vision of the whole of life. Sexuality, polarity, magnetism and reciprocal relationships of all kinds will be perceived as governing forces through all levels of life and matter, and love itself will be seen as a cosmic necessity . . . .

The joyful practices of Fantasy and prolonged intercourse, the erotic massage and psychic energization, and the psychological awakening and re-birth that these practices engender are all lovingly and beautifully developed in this book — but they are just the 'foreplay' to the rituals of "Cosmic Awareness Intercourse" fully described in Chapter 8, and then developed still further in Chapter 9 as "The Ritual of Sex Magick for the Conception of a Child" and "The Ritual of Sex Magick to Achieve Material Objectives."

Sex Magick, through Cosmic Awareness Intercourse, takes effect by bringing into action the beneficient forces of the Universe — of which there is abundance to supply the needs of all. You are taught how to make

Sex the core of your marriage, and the foundation for the success of that partnership at all levels of your lives. You will be channeling the Divine Radiance through yourselves, and this will enhance your health, and charge everything you do with Power and Beauty.

Again, we can make no better description of the ideas involved in the Magical Conception of a Child than our authors, who write:

The conception of a child, considered as an act of Sex Magick, is the highest, most natural and logical form of that art. In determining and bringing about the result, the partners unite to produce, in the material world, a living expression of their love and their power, an indivisible token of their oneness.

The conception of a child through Cosmic Awareness Intercourse, when both parents are practiced and proficient in that rite, is a spiritual act of special welcome for that child, creating at once an ambience of supreme blessing, of equilibrium and of harmonious good at every level for the person who comes into incarnation in these conditions.

But, just as Sex is for us more than the means to the birth of a child, so is marriage much more than a social, or legal, institution. *The Magick of Sex* shows the many ways in which sexual loving becomes a means to the psychological growth and full realization of the inner maturity of man and woman. In addition, there is a long and glorious mystical tradition in the West that is based less on sex as symbol than on the full know-ledge of sex as alchemy!

Our authors show how the Qabalah — that complete transmission of the Western Tradition — completely describes the process of Creation, and the Path of Return. Here we have the true nature of the psyche and of the Universe; the force and the form of all that is; the glory of the Cosmic Drama and the essence of all human history that is past and yet to come. And all that is the Qabalah is 'condensed' into the picture-formula known as "The Tree of Life."

The Book of Genesis (1:27) says:

And God created man in His own image, in the image of God created He him: male and female created He them.

Male and female, *together,* are the image of the Creator, and in the Tree of Life may be found under-standing of this ultimate mystery. Our book says:

The plan of the whole Tree of Life is set for each person to integrate inwardly through life's experiences; but the Tree represents life in its entirety, both in its male and its female aspects. It follows, therefore, that Man will find some of its lessons harder to learn, while Woman will have difficulty with others.

If, however, the man and the woman unite their powers, finding through sexual love the ability to create a united identity and thus to make each other's life-experience their own, then together they have the key to every mystery.

The Magick of Sex can become a complete Path of

Magical and Spiritual Attainment, for it is through Yesod — the Moon Sphere — that the Way of Return leads. Here is the realm of dreams, fantasy, psychism and sexuality. And here, as the Tree of Life shows, male and female are united — and in this level of being place is given to both principles (of masculinity and femininity) in each person.

And it is from Yesod that the Path to the Stars is opened. The descent of the Star Fire in the lovers opens the way for their ascent to the power and glory that is the realization of their Divinity — and it is that for which we are born!

Carl Llewellyn Weschcke
Publisher

Contents

sight! A new level of experience for the couple. *Rediscovering the fantasy games of the troubadours.* The medieval synthesis of cultures. The new face of sexual love: the supremacy of "unconsummated" devotion. Fantasy lovers weren't supposed to be married to each other. The true meaning and magical importance of this convention. Parallels in a mystical cult of Krishna. Main purpose of fantasy and role-playing in the Magick of Sex clearly shown: release from mundane circumstances into the adventure of love freely given. The "pure love" of the troubadours compared to results of ejaculation control. *Have joy in what you do.* Outlines of troubadour fantasies: You and your lover are parted (The Bridge of Desire, and the Rescue Game); Mistress (or Master) and Slave; Deity and Worshiper; The Chastity Pact.

8 **Cosmic Awareness Intercourse**
Sexual experience an initiation. Glimpsing your partner's higher self: the person you really love, a true fragment of the Divine Mind. *You and your partner can worship the Divine in each other — can worship each other body and soul, as irradiated by the higher self.* Survey of preparation through the Magick of Sex which is needed for this rite. *Step-by-step account of Cosmic Awareness Intercourse:* the first visualizations, the adoration, the energizer, the sexual actions, use of three Centers of Activity, techniques of visualization and timed breathing during intercourse. The mystical kiss and the culminating acts. The kiss as an aid to mystical

Study Points

1

1. The power inherent in Love/Sex/Romance is a *creative magical force* underlying every facet of Life — from the physical level through the highest reaches of spirit.

2. This same power should be made a vital source of renewal and development in your personal life. "Sexual love is a way to the heights."

3. This book is a couples' book! This power can be used to realize the full potential that lies in the relationship between a man and a woman — joining them together at every level of their psyches.

   a. This integration of two persons into one whole also brings about the integration of levels within each that is the goal of all pyschological growth and work.

1

b. Powerful as it is — this power that brings two people together — it is perfected through conscious effort. This is the subject matter of the book. So effective, however, are the techniques taught here that they can be initiated by one of the partners; so powerful is the Magick of Sex that it can work for one person alone to build his or her inner life so as to attract a mate.

4. Sex is not limited to, nor dependent upon, physical sexual action! And even if sex does not have a physical place in your life, it can and should be given an emotional and spiritual place, and will, then, lead to happiness, growth and integration.

a. The physical level of sex, by itself, is not sufficient to give lasting happiness, nor to keep a relationship between a man and a woman alive and vital.

b. Physical actions can, however, become the means for bringing about inner development and integration: it is the consciously directed physical act, carried out with awareness of the psychic side, that is the magical tool to transform the present into the sought-after ideal.

5. We are — each of us — in the depths of our psyche both male and female, Animus and Anima; and it is the principle opposite to that which is dominant in our conscious personality that is projected on to the beloved person.

a. In addition to the great male and female aspects

within the psyche, for each of us — no matter which is our personal sex —there is a sense in which our physical body is "female" to our conscious and purposeful psyche; and in which our emotional and instinctive nature is "female" to our "male" intellect, and in which the entire lower nature, including the intellect, is "female" to the Higher Self.

b. By bringing harmony and purpose into our outer world activities, we bring harmony to the inner levels — making them "fertile" to the inspiration of the Higher Self.

c. By working to build a good Love/Sex/Romance relationship we use the most powerful means to achieving inner harmony and realization, and to tapping the fullness of our inner resources for conscious purpose whether in the inner or the outer worlds.

6. This wonderful, magical, relationship between parents is vital to the wholesome development of the child. What is shared between parents acts as a "pattern" for the growth and development of the child. Bringing a child into the world should be a conscious, willfull action in which the responsibilities of parenthood are realized, desired, and accepted.

7. *Awareness of the sexual significance in a shared action between the partners is the secret of the*

magical relationship. Learn to use your imagination to feel and perceive as your partner does, and make use of this knowledge in indulging your partner's particular "turn-ons," in responding to your partner's romantic-needs, in meeting your partner's love-needs.

a. This use of the imagination will not only increase your partner's pleasures and depth of sexual experience, but your own as well.

b. Learning to use your imagination in this way to identify with your partner's experience and expression brings your inner, opposite sexual nature into balance with your outer sexual being. It's part of true maturity.

c. Even without physical level sexual expression, this experience can become an intense spiritual experience as can be seen in the lives of such Western mystics as St. John of the Cross and St. Teresa of Avila.

d. This mystical and spiritual aspect of the inner worlds of sexual experience will be explored further in later chapters. It will be seen to be indeed magical — rich in its power to bring sexuality into full flower, rich in its power to strengthen the relationship between the partners, rich in its power to grace the world.

1

The Magick of Sex

Love — sex — romance! These are among the most intensely magical things in life, life's most potent forces. They have been potent in building up or transforming whole cultures; they have been, and can always be, potent in building up or in refashioning the life of any person. *They can be, and should be, a vital factor, a source of constant renewal and inner development, in your own life.*

This is a force essentially creative, not only at the wonderful physical level, but at all other levels of human life so that even the rational intellect is warmed and enlightened by its power. Art and literature are filled with it; even the highest utterances of mysticism and spirituality would have been poorer, or in many cases impossible, without the imagery and the insights of sexual love. The lives of countless millions of people have been illuminated with added meaning by it, given inspiration and aspiration. It has opened gateways for them into other worlds of experience maybe not consciously recognized: gateways even to the world of the Divine.

This is not only a matter of emotional and physical pleasure, important though that is. It involves also the integration, over time, of a man and a woman through their sexual partnership; their fulfillment at all levels by and through that partnership. That, basically, is what a lasting relationship is about; what it can and should be about, whether it started as a love-affair, a bid for security, a desire to raise children, or anything else involving mutual goodwill and the intention of staying together on an intimate basis. Sexual love is a way to the heights.

In this day and age it can be said that pretty well any couple who set up a lasting relationship either love each other, or have loved each other, or have the potential to love each other. This book is for all those people: for all those people their partnership can be a supreme source of happiness, if they will mutually try to make it so. It can mean literally *incredible* happiness!

Even those who have but lately fallen in love may not realize how much joy, bliss, rapture at all levels their life together can hold!

In a sense, everybody knows about what we are saying here. It's the Love Dream; a blending of physical and emotional and spiritual joy shared by two people in a special way. Once it starts, it goes on without end. Only sometimes people fall out of it, or don't have the key to it, or because of past disenchantments they feel it isn't for them. Yet it's all there as it has been through untold ages of human experience, and as it has been known and handed down for many centuries in our own Western Mystery Tradition — all the magick and wonder, all the deep mysticism and the simple inexpressible joy. It's there for you and your partner; and there are many keys to it.

Two things, however, are certain about this way to happiness. One is, no matter how blessed you are in your love to begin with, if you want that happiness to last more than a few years you and your partner have to put your will and understanding into keeping and increasing it; But the other thing is, no matter how far a partnership may have broken down in disputes, in coldness or in seeming apathy — or if from any cause the physical relationship seems completely ended — yet, if both partners want to make the effort, and if both will begin the new venture on the love-sex level, that venture can become a radiant success in their lives. *In many cases, this radiant success can follow even when initially it's* only ONE partner *who sincerely wishes to build it up!* — or, so powerful is this Magick of Sex, it can work for one person alone who wants to build his or her inner life so as to attract a mate.

It's true that sex, *in the sense of physical sexual action,* does not play a leading part in every person's life. Some very great men and women, and also many unknown people, have lived in quite another way, whether by choice or through force of circumstances. Many married couples, even, have for one reason or another to forego complete physical union for a longer or shorter span of time. We say, however, that in the lives of all these people, married or not, if they are to be happy, balanced and creative adults, the *foundations* of sexual love have to be recognized.

If sex is not given a physical place in our lives, happiness and integration are still possible *if sex is given its rightful emotional and spiritual place;* and, likewise, in the lives of people who have every physical gratification, the material level alone is not enough to give lasting happiness *unless there is also emotional and spiritual fulfillment.* For in fact true happiness can only be ours when we are growing towards (and when we attain) the maturation and the inner integration of our psyche.

We have to consider how we can best ensure this development and harmony within.

Most people achieve their inner development by dealing with concerns in the material world which can reflect the great psychic processes (whether we perceive this or not) and then bringing those material concerns to their own right balance and harmony. As an example:

the graphologists tell us how our various character traits, pleasing and otherwise, are all reflected in our handwriting. In some ways this makes us vulnerable, because a prospective employer (for instance) only needs to get an expert to look at our handwriting to find out quite a lot about us, but in other ways it gives us a very powerful instrument to use for our own benefit. If we have a trait of character which we'd be better without, for instance, a good way to set about making the change is to find out what are the "symptoms" of that trait as shown in our handwriting, and then to take advice on how best to improve the writing. This can take a fair amount of patience and practice, but is frequently very effective in de-fusing the cause of the trouble.

Likewise, if you want to stop losing your temper with certain people, you can begin by leaving off clenching your fists and shouting when this happens!

Where your inner nature leads, your outer nature will follow. *But also, where your outer nature leads your inner nature will follow:* and this is usually the easier way to get results.

When it comes to working towards one's inner integration, many people are knowingly or unknowingly helped by some daily activity, their work or, often, a hobby. The objects which occupy them in the material world can reflect, one way or another, some of the great psychic processes, and when in the normal course of events these people bring the object of their activity to a right balance and harmony, *that balance and harmony becomes part of their own inner experience.* Not only the artist, the musician and the craftsperson do this in their special ways, but also the horticulturist, the teacher, the athlete do it (with living materials!)

The architect and the builder can achieve it, and that realization has given its symbolism to Masonry. The scientific researcher too can bring about the same thing, and this was discovered long ago by the Alchemists.

ALL WHO CONCERN THEMSELVES WITH MATERIALS, LIVING OR OTHERWISE, IN THE WORLD AROUND THEM AND WHO STRIVE TO BRING THOSE MATERIALS TO A HIGHER DEVELOPMENT OR TO ESTABLISH FOR THEM TRUE PATTERNS AND HARMONIES, WILL FIND THEM-SELVES OVER A PERIOD OF TIME IDENTIFYING WITH WHAT THEY ARE DOING: THEY WILL FIND THEY HAVE ALSO BROUGHT BALANCE AND HARMONY AND HIGHER DEVELOPMENT INTO THEIR OWN PSYCHE.

To co-ordinate color and form on canvas brings co-ordination into the soul of the painter; to awaken aspiration in a pupil likewise confirms that aspiration in the teacher. In this, as we sow so shall we assuredly reap, for we sow both outwardly and inwardly at the same time.

How vitally, therefore, we are moving towards our inner fulfillment and integration when we concern our-selves at the interpersonal level with the working out

*of harmonies and relationships in the sphere of sex,
since we know, and the psychologists have amply
demonstrated, what paramount components of our
inner life correspond to the roles of sexuality!*

For every individual, there are present to the
depths of the psyche two great archetypal forces,
corresponding to the Supernal Father and the Supernal
Mother: Animus and Anima. Carl Jung, whose books
give a great deal of attention to these forces, describes
them as "autonomous complexes," meaning that there
is nothing we can do about them directly by means of
our conscious mind: it's of no use to *will* them to do or
not do this or that, or to be or not be this or that.
The normal adult development is for the conscious
personality of a man to identify more or less with the
Animus principle, the conscious personality of a woman
to identify more or less with the Anima principle, so
that those images become "invisible" to their bearers.
(We don't, for instance, usually dream about seeing
ourselves, except perhaps in a mirror.) The other,
latent, Archetype — the Anima in a man, the Animus
in a woman — is then likely to be "projected", in the
psychological sense, on to some other person of suitable
sex and other characteristics; that person then becomes
beloved, or even spontaneously "adored," but not
always seen in a very objective way.

Of course, the situation may not be either as spontaneous as that or a simple as that. Not even the most

"macho man" identifies 100% with the Animus, nor the most feminine woman 100% with the Anima. There are besides Animus and Anima many other factors introduced by heredity or by experience into the psyche to make us just the persons we are. Again, we can *project* many other elements of our psychic make-up besides those two, and our impressions of our friends and acquaintences, relatives and love-partners will be varied accordingly, with the subjective "lens" through which we see them.

Too, besides the great male and female components in our psyche which exist side by side as it were — the active and latent aspects of our sexuality — there is also a sexually-toned inter-relationship between the different levels of our being. Thus, no matter which is our personal sex, we can regard our body as "female" in relation to the directing and impregnating psyche. It is Shakespeare's Richard II who says,

My brain I'll prove the female to my soul,
My soul the father; and these two beget
A generation of still-breeding thoughts . . .

(King Richard II, Act V, scene 5.)

Or, again, within our psyche, we can regard our emotional-instinctual nature as "female", and our intellect as "male" in relation to that. But also (and this is very important) the whole of our lower nature, *including the intellect,* is "female," in the sense not only of "passive" but chiefly as "fertile", "bringing-forth-into-manifestation", when it is impregnated by the inspiring Spirit, the Higher Self.

This whole chain of development is dependent on reactions which, so far as our human life is concerned, are *reactions to sexuality.* If we despise one or other of the sexes, or if we resent or fear one or the other, or if we despair of their ability to interact peaceably and productively — if we prefer to keep all functions in neatly-analyzed compartments — then we are inhibiting the life-processes of our own inner nature.

We can't get directly at these deep unconscious levels of ourselves to make adjustments. What we have to do is to put the conscious outer levels, and the physical level, the body, into order; and doing this will resonate the deeper levels in their true and life-giving patterns.

To do this effectively, we need to give our attention wholly and genuinely to our outer-world activities. It's fortunate that building a good love-sex relationship is a fairly absorbing occupation, since inner psychological and spiritual progress is a plant which will not thrive if its roots are continually being pulled up for examination.

If you like, you can say that what this Practical Guide gives is a kind of sexual Masonry, or sexual Alchemy. Both of these would be true descriptions, although we shall proceed in a quite non-formal way.

The inner forces of sex are sacred! One of the greatest mystics of the western world in near-modern times, Saint John of the Cross, was a Carmelite monk living in the 16th century. His career was devoted to the monastic life and to bringing his Order into line with that ideal as he saw it. He was assuredly a true ascetic, but it was not this by itself which made him a saint or a mystic. He was a complete human being, with a deep awareness of the material world and of the inter-relationship of the two sexes at the various levels of being.

If his celibacy had been prompted by an aversion to women, he could not have benefited (as he very greatly did) from the friendship, ideas and inspirations of Saint Teresa of Avila, who was a spiritual mother to him. If he had been hostile to sexuality, he could not have composed his wonderful poems, which set forth the high experience of love and union with God in terms of human love and union. Some of these poems he based on the popular love-songs of Spain, and one magnificent dialogue-canticle he based on the Song of Solomon. They are intensely sensuous in their imagery without being sensual, intensely lyrical in form and spirit yet full of profound implications.

Nobody could have written as he did unless entirely convinced that sexual love could give a worthy and appropriate representation of the most sublime spiritual experiences. *Nor would those poems have been possible, either, but for a real relationship existing between the earthly and the mystical levels of experience.* But we shall return to some parallels between mystical and sexual experience, and their exciting sginificance for earthly lovers, later in this book.

There is another angle, too, on developing the marital relationship to its full potential of love and sexual happiness. This relationship is, admittedly, a charmed circle enclosing the man and the woman and none other. Their children are truly "outside" it; but the children cannot be otherwise than aware of it, to a degree which will increase with their own development but which has probably always a strong unconscious component. *And what a wonderful gift the presence of this relationship can form for the children!* Because it exists, an abundance of love will radiate to them, so they will have no cause to feel "rejected" or resentful about this special thing between father and mother. Instead, they will know there is something wonderful reserved for adulthood, the like of which they can look forward to in times to come, in their own adult life.

This is important. Childhood is a marvelous time. Bodily energy usually seems inexhaustible; growth, increasing strength and dexterity, increasing knowledge and mental abilities not only come of their own accord bringing enjoyment and exhilaration, but they earn praise as well. Not only the outer but also the inner faculties are intensely acute and aware; the imagination gives an extra dimension to every kind of activity, while psychism and make-believe mutually widen each other's boundaries without stint. What do the children see adults enjoying in exchange for this world of growth, development and wonder?

One does sometimes meet children who seem in some subtle way *afraid to grow up;* children to whom every blessing seems to come while they are small, children who see in the lives of the adults around them nothing but worries and responsiblitities, anxieties and disagreements. In such a view of life, all the privileges can seem to belong to childhood.

No matter whether you have much or little of worldly goods, in this most important respect you can give your children the prospect of a supremely happy future of a quality which neither riches nor education can ensure: a joyful, lasting and fulfilling marriage experience. *Nor will this be merely a good image for them to strive consciously for. The unconscious mind takes a vital part in this.*

Research constantly shows that the psyche, especially in childhood, is quick to take the experiences of the present as patterns for the future. Some almost bizarre histories could be cited, of how people have striven in adult life to avoid repeating a woeful pattern of behavior set by the parents, only to be trapped into that same pattern by seeming chance, a network of "happenstance" which in truth was woven or attracted by the victim's unconscious mind. It is supremely important, therefore, above all in the essential matter of sexual relationships, to give a good, happy *and genuine* image to be built into your children's conscious and unconscious impressions of what goes on around them; and, most fortunately, this is one area of life WHICH YOU CAN DIRECT, even when other circumstances — health, prosperity and the rest — may show distinct room for improvement. *Give your children this, and you are truly enhancing their own prospects of marital happiness, and of inner integration, in the future.*

You owe it to yourself, to your partner and to your children, then, to make the most and the best of your sex-life, to discover and to live out the real magick of being an adult. Only in a lasting relationship can the quest of the Magick of Sex be fully and successfully carried out. It needs self-understanding, and it needs understanding of one's partner.

We are writing for the couple whose relationship has, or is to be given, reality and stability. There should be an intention in both partners to build up the relationship into something continually stronger and deeper, with a real desire to find more happiness, spiritual and emotional fulfillment, physical pleasure and — of course — downright fun in each other's company. That doesn't cut out any other reasons you may have for wanting your relationship to be a success: in fact, the more motivations you have, the better!

Although you will in this way be creating a unique life-work, and although we shall describe several different approaches to the love-sex relationship, there are some

general guide-lines which can be mentioned before
going on to the particulars.

Certainly good sex is possible without love, and
great love is possible and often exists without sex; but
love in a sexual relationship is without compare, and is
the ideal for lasting union, a true way to the heights.

Not that there should be too much "pushing" for
either ingredient, sex or love. Worry, anxiety, stress, are
NOT the way it's done! *Don't worry* about multiple
orgasms, or even about achieving *one* on any given
occasion. Equally, *don't worry* about whether you love
your partner enough, or whether he or she loves you
enough. *Above all, don't make a habit of asking! Give*
assurances of love when you feel like it or when the
relationship needs it. *Court* your partner (yes, even after
ten, twenty, thirty-plus years together!) but don't
habitually ask whether you are loved: *cultivate an ambience of love and dwell in it.*

The important thing is for both partners to *enjoy*
the relationship. Do nothing which will lessen your own
or your partner's pleasure, do all you can to enhance it.
Enjoy and be happy!

This involves finding means of realization and
expression for what is already there, physically, emotionally and spiritually; it involves feeling for, and with, the
person who both gives and shares the experience: the
person whom you are to perceive, when this realization
is fully developed, as truly your other self. It involves

giving time, thought and place in your life to this intimate inter-relationship as the essential part of your life which it is.

Devoting due time and attention to the love-sex relationship in this way gives a couple a much-needed "oasis," a sphere of inter-communication which is far above and apart from the outer-world levels at which they maybe disagree, bicker or have quite different interests and occupations from each other. Certainly the intimate side of their life will blossom and will spill over its sweetness into the other occupations, but the other occupations should never be allowed to intrude, however peaceably, into their love-life.

IT SHOULD BE A FIRM RULE FOR BOTH OF THE PARTNERS THAT NO MENTION OF ANY SUCH OUTSIDE MATTERS IS TO BE MADE DURING THEIR SESSIONS OF LOVEMAKING.

NEITHER, HOWEVER, SHOULD ONE EVER BEGIN, OR PROPOSE LOVE-MAKING, DELIBERATELY AS A PLOY TO END A SERIOUS DISCUSSION ON OTHER MATTERS. THAT IS AN EVEN GREATER SACRILEGE AGAINST SEXUAL LOVE, AND CAN TURN A RELATIONSHIP TO DUST AND ASHES.

As lovers, you and your partner have much to explore! Beware of short cuts, and of feeling you know each other's "turn-ons". You may both be missing all kinds of exciting possiblities. Human beings are complex creatures, and freshness, change and novelty are themselves great attractions! From time to time, certainly, it's reassuring and nostalgic to slip back into old accustomed ways; but even in that there would be no nostalgia, no sense of homecoming, if you never departed from that routine.

Whatever you do or experience in your partner's company which has any sexual significance — whether you give or receive a caress, or put on or take off a garment, or listen to sensuous music, or burn an incense stick — *make it a shared experience!* While you are experiencing it yourself, make an effort to realize and feel, *in your imagination*, the way your partner is experiencing it.

DO THIS ESPECIALLY DURING INTERCOURSE, BUT BE CAREFUL TO DO IT ALSO DURING OTHER SHARED EXPERIENCES.

Never mind the fact that a lot of your partner's minor experiences will be identical, or nearly so, with your own; still, after letting it register in your own senses, nervous system, mind, body, relate it to your partner and imagine the effect of it to your partner's different senses, nervous system, mind, body. This imaginative practice can be brought to a high degree of reality, since, both in the psyche and the body, *each sex has, latently, the characteristics of the other.*

It is by using these latent faculties of your own with reference to your partner, that you will develop completeness in your own sexual awareness while keeping your sexual orientation clear.

You will enhance both your own and your partner's pleasure: your own pleasure because your imagination will enable you to enjoy your partner's pleasure besides that which you have in your own right, and your partner's pleasure because all your sexual actions will be better planned and better timed if you make the effort to imagine their effect.

You will also be helping yourself towards psychic maturity. Let's make this clearer by considering the sexual development of the psyche in more detail.

There is no need here to go into the psychological stages of develpment of young children. We need only say as a brief generalization that there is a tendency in both boys and girls, from about eight years old to puberty, to spend as much time as they can in the company of a group of friends of, mainly, their own sex. They are developing their own conscious personality and their social image, and while they are about these considerable tasks they appreciate the company of their similars. (Most people keep something of this tendency throughout life, and like to brush up their social image from time to time by talk with, and observation of, their similars in sex, age and occupation. Without this, they might find themselves on the knife-edge of standing as trend-setters or falling perhaps as eccentrics!) In children, this phase usually passes into the "best friend" stage when enough individuality has been developed to make such choices, and when the co-operation and support of only a like-minded few is needed or desired.

When the young person's conscious personality is well established, friendship of course continues but its protective function is not so much required. The adolescent is then ready for the next stage, the company of the opposite sex.

It should be borne in mind that during the years of preparation which we have described, the opposite-sex characteristics in the adolescent's own psyche have usually been firmly and progressively relegated to its unconscious levels. That is quite in order.

It is precisely because those opposite-sex characteristics are there, *and are unconscious,* that the adolescent is able to fall in love with a person who possesses those characteristics. Almost inevitably, by the time a boy or a girl reaches adolescence a lot of qualities besides those belonging to the opposite sex have also been pushed down into the unconscious, and these other qualities too are likely to influence the choice of a "first love". Hence problems sometimes arise with regard to teenage attachments; problems which don't appear earlier when young children solemnly choose (as they sometimes do) a "girl friend" or a "boy friend". The reason for the difference is that with young children the unconscious levels are not involved in the choice to the same extent: they may seem more "sensible" than their teenage brothers and sisters, but, by the same token, they are "too young to fall in love."

In early adult life, then, it is suitable for the sexual partners to be as "different" from one another as possible. To play down the "otherness" is to declare a "truce area" of life, in which, for purposes of study, sport, business or other special activity, sex at any level is understood to be kept out of the picture. Conversely, at other times, differences are *emphasized;* not only with reference to the partner, but also for each person's own enjoyment and pride in role-playing.

This, however, could end in a mutual incomprehension which would not make for good sharing in love or good pyschological development. *Having effectively separated Animus from Anima within ourselves — a vital early stage — we have to bring them together within ourselves, in harmonious union.* That is essential for our psychic well-being in a balanced, creative and fulfilling maturity.

In the man, Anima has the function of bringing such qualities as tenderness, romance and love of beauty into the strength and intellectualism of his life, and of giving him an understanding of woman.

In the woman, Animus has the function of bringing such qualities as order, reason and direction into the intuitiveness and the emotional flow of her life, and of giving her an understanding of man.

A person in whom these opposite-sex attributes did not appear would be living only half a life. A person in whom these opposite-sex attributes run wild — an over-emotional man or a hard unfeeling woman — likewise does not have the conscious and unconscious functions harmoniously united within.

Some people have a degree of mature Anima-Animus balance from an early age. They are generally remarkable people in one way or another, although in extreme cases they can miss out completely on the experience of falling in love.

The artist or the otherwise creative man or woman who rises above mediocrity — the "genius type" — always does so by the power and co-operativeness of the opposite-sex function in his or her psyche. Naturally, this is not equally observable in every instance, but it is frequently unmistakeable.

The friendship of John of the Cross and Teresa of Avila has already been mentioned. We can consider them both at this point.

The reforms to which John devoted his life were originally of Teresa's planning. He showed great courage and patience under persecution and physical suffering, of which he had a notable share. He possessed keen spiritual perception and an inflexible will to keep to his chosen course, but also a most tender compassion for others and a gift for spiritual poetry of the utmost romantic and sensuous feeling.

Teresa was a Carmelite nun who experienced visions and levitation, but she was by no means a recluse; she took a very energetic part in all that concerned her or her work. Her writings are conspicuous in religious literature, not only for their deep spiritual content but for their practical common sense, shrewd self-observation and sparkling humor. *Her genius exemplifies the guiding spirit of Animus as surely as John's exemplifies that of the Anima.*

The way of celibacy has never been for more than a minority of men and women; *but to integrate the dual sexual components in the psyche is the need of all who would reach a true adulthood.*

Active sexual life too has its modes of mysticism, which are open to all who seek them: *and for most people a clear way to attain both maturity and mystical awareness, and much more besides, is mapped out through the stabilizing, joyful and inspiring influence of a happy sexual partnership.*

Don't let anyone attempt to make you feel guilty or ashamed of your sexuality! In man or woman it is strength and beauty and joy, and can remain so from youth into age. There are people who seem to think men and women get married in order to *give up* sex, or at least to give up any outward manifestation of it. Don't heed such people; why should the living-out of the great physical and psychic patterns be anything else than joyful?

Of course, there are aspects of sexual love which call for serious thought and great personal responsibility. *Promising love and fidelity to someone* is one of these aspects: *you should be sure both of you really mean the same things by it!* — and bringing a child into the world is another: *that's something no civilized person should do without good will and good hope for the child's future.* It would be a poor gift to the person who comes first in your life, to make him or her an unwilling and maybe a totally unready parent.

Besides, no matter how Fortune might subsequently smile upon the child, life often keeps a very bitter kernel for the unwelcome. A young child can pick up, without words and even before birth, an awareness of having through its coming spoiled the life of a parent, for instance, or of having been brought into a bad heritage into which a loving father and mother would never have called anyone. Such an awareness can open up in the depths of the child's psyche a deep well of self-scorn and self-hatred, all the more potent because unavowed. People who have been taught to regard "self-love" as selfishness may find it difficult to realize *that there is a self-love which is a necessary condition for right living;* we must desire the greatest good for ourselves, and what we desire for ourselves is what we will desire for others.

Those who hate or despise themselves will project hatred and contempt all around them, and the world as a whole suffers for it. These truths are not often uttered, but they need to be stated here: we all have a grave responsibility, to bring children into the world only in conditions of real love and caring.

Of course, we don't have to be perfectionists, or to wait for a family until we can bring our children into our middle-life affluence; but among the qualities required for good parenthood are love, loyalty and prudence, and there is no substitute for them.

If you need to use a technique of contraception and you have full confidence in your method, keep to it; if you don't altogether feel like trusting any *one* way — and few claim 100% safety — then get advice from your local Family Planning organization about *two* which will work well together (such as a gel and a sheath). Any initial embarrassment in using contraceptives will disappear with habitude, and will be more than compensated by the sense of freedom and relaxation in which you and your partner can then take your pleasure together.

Checkpoint

1

- The partnership of man and woman should bring about their integration, both person to person and inwardly for each.

- Goodwill and understanding are the partners' basic needs, whether they desire to keep and increase their present happiness or to rebuild a damaged relationship.

- The emotional and spiritual levels of sexuality are vital for EVERYONE. If physical sex isn't here and now possible for you, cultivating those non-physical levels can still safeguard your psychological wholeness; whereas no amount of physical sex will bring true happiness if the inner levels are lacking.

- *Where your outer nature leads, your inner nature will follow.* So, if you work at strengthening your sex-love relationship with your partner, you'll be building towards integrating the deep levels of your own psyche. *(Besides making your partner happy!)*

- To do this effectively, keep your attention upon the outer-world action: *don't uproot your inner life for inspection!*

- The example of happy and fulfilled adulthood in Mother and Father is a wonderful gift for your children!

- Put all you can into your love-sex relationship, but don't worry about high physical or emotional achievement. *You are creating a unique life-work.* Enjoy and be happy!

- Love and sex are a sacred part of your life. Don't let other concerns intrude into your love-making sessions! And never *use* love-making as a tool to evade other topics.

- You've probably submerged and even forgotten opposite-sex characteristics you had as a small child. Now you need to find those, or similar, characteristics *in your partner*, and, through sexual love, participate in them yourself.

- Make your own observation of sexual balance as it is frequently shown in the work of outstanding people: men and women dedicated to a religion, to an art, or to any great cause.

- Active sexual life is a way of attainment, having its own mysticism and its own paths to the heights of human experience. *Be conscious of the dignity and the validity of the sexual way.*

Study Points
2

1. Sharing, in the relationship between a man and a
   woman, is a demand upon your own self-awareness
   and honesty, and upon your awareness and perception of your partner's unconscious as well as consciously expressed needs and desires.
   a. Bring into conscious awareness as much as possible
      concerning your Love/Sex/Romance relationship.
      Deliberately look for meanings and motivations in
      body language, inflections of voice, spontaneous
      actions.
   b. Share personal decisions — almost always they
      have some effect on your partner. When not shared,
      they may be misunderstood and become a source
      of tension between the two of you.
   c. Each of you must stop taking yourself for granted!
      Learn to see yourself through the eyes of the other,

and seek to present yourself in a clear and exciting image.

   d. Later chapters will help show you how to explore different facets of your own and your partner's personality.

2. Just as within each of us there is Anima and Animus, so is there the archetype of the Eternal Child (not to be confused with "childishness").

   a. While it is often difficult to perceive the Child in oneself, and even in other people of the same sex it is easier for men to see it in women, and for women to see it in men — and especially so in the case of one's mate.

   b. Learn to look upon the Eternal Child with respect and appreciation: it is an important part of our total being.

   c. This archetype of the Eternal Child must, too, be brought into harmony with the other aspects of your psyche, and it is the sexual relationship which creates a special intimacy in which we can recapture the magick, the creativity, the fun of childhood.

3. Love/Sex/Romance all deserve a special "openness" between the partners. Complete union is inhibited when one or both partners withhold aspects of themselves from the other. Learn to think even that your body is as much your partner's as your own. Be "as a

garment to one another!"

a. Be open in expressing sexual pleasure, and in exploring each other's bodies — and in accepting the caresses your partner enjoys giving you.

b. Try to imagine what the other feels; learn to enjoy the other's pleasure in a caress given as in a caress received.

c. Openness also means to be non-demanding.
"Not every love-session need end in sexual union."
"Not every sexual union need end in ejaculation."
Love and sexuality have many modes of expression, and none need be consummated on a time-schedule, nor only at the physical level.

4. In following the teachings of the Magick of Sex, you will build your relationship body to body, *and* instinct to instinct, emotion to emotion, mind to mind, and spirit to spirit.

a. Not only are these relationships built, over time, through sharing, but these contacts between levels of being can be instituted through special *psychophysical energizers* that can be made part of a program of exchanging energies as well as physical contacts.

b. These energizers depend upon "visualization" to stimulate the movement of natural currents that flow in and around the body.

c. These energizers are pleasurable parts of foreplay to love-making, useful before other activities, and valuable in psycho-magical techniques for activating the *chakras:* those great gateways by and through which the Life-force is channeled.

d. The special energizers here described as a series of psycho-physical visualizations and movements are made more powerful by being shared between sexual partners than equivalent exercises intended for individual use.

e. As will be seen later, they play a very important role in psycho-spiritual development.

2

Reciprocal Energies

In all human relationships the body is our primary means of communication. The body speaks even in our silence; consciously and unconsciously we give impressions to other people, consciously and unconsciously we receive impressions from them. Our conscious mind, and theirs, may be too unskilled — or too tolerant — to take much notice of some of the information thus received; but our unconscious minds are registering impressions all the time, and are interpreting them at sub-rational level. Our relationships are frequently influenced in this way by our favorable or adverse responses to stimuli which we hadn't consciously even noticed we received.

This applies very much to our relationship with people we've known for some time, and especially with our intimate partner.

Your conscious mind may have ceased to notice

many facts about a person seen every day, but your unconscious mind will pick up details continually and your relationship with that person is likely to be influenced accordingly, often without your conscious mind even noticing what's happening. This is one of the reasons, and a very practical reason, for bringing as much as possible concerning your love-sex relationship into consciousness: your own and/or your partner's consciousness, as circumstances may require.

As a simple example: A woman may feel she can help the household budget by going without some beauty aid which her man never seems to notice she uses. In spite of his lack of conscious perceptiveness about the way she enhances her appearance, however, it's a good thing if she lets him share her decision.

This is not only so he can positively *appreciate* her action. She might feel she could forego that; but, much more important, her telling him will prevent any possible *hurt* he might feel, if he merely picked up an uncomprehended impression that she wasn't bothering quite so much these days to make herself attractive for him.

When you are with someone you have only just met, the whole business of impression giving and taking is intensified on each side and at all levels, conscious and other. There is no warrant for the popular belief that first impressions are always accurate (in the sense of being correctly interpreted) but they are certainly

extremely powerful. They are not, however, our problem
here. What we are concerned with is the question of
how someone can continue presenting an equally
vivid picture to his or her permanent partner, receiving
also a clear and exciting image of the partner in return.

Some of the ways are such common-sense Magick
as to seem perhaps obvious, but they are of prime
importance all the same. *Each partner should stop
taking himself or herself for granted, then the other
will likewise cease to take him or her for granted.*

This book will give suggestions for games and
for various play-situations, each allowing you to explore
different facets of your own and your partner's personality. The self-preparation for these games will give you
fresh incentives for renewed attention to your physical
appearance, your voice, your manner, in one way or
another; you will make the best of this or that aspect
of yourself, you and your partner will take renewed
pleasure in looking at each other and in being looked
at by each other, and each of you will find new attractions
and associations with the other in consequence.

In this present chapter however we are concerned
with the discovery of self and of the partner at a
particularly deep and essential level. Certainly you can,
and should, use the techniques to be given here as a
prelude to love-making, but also you can use them any
time you want for other purposes: when one or both
of you feel threatened by worry or anxiety, when one

is tired (or, in some cases, when both are), when for any reason loving care seems more to be desired than immediate ecstasy.

Even while you are making love, you should never forget the importance of the less specialized forms of bodily contact. Passionate kisses don't obviate more tender ones, and sexual contacts don't take the place of simple, loving, caring caresses. There is a sentence in the Quran which states that husband and wife should be *as a garment to one another;* this eloquently expresses the feeling of comfort and protection, quite apart from sexual rapture, which man and woman need from one another.

When we are growing up, it is through the development of sexuality that we cease to be children. We need to become adults in our daily work, in our sense of responsibility and in our emotional control. We become adult in the maturation and development of the lower regions of the psyche; we should also become adult in our awareness of the upper regions of the psyche, doing what seems right because we inwardly recognize it as our way, not just because we are obedient or afraid of punishment.

All these developments will help us towards maturity, *but they don't blot out the child which remains, however submerged, in each person.* To put it in terms of Jungian psychology, just as Anima and Animus are great archetypes which are beyond the control of our conscious will, and to which we have to establish a satisfactory relationship, so also is the archetype of the Eternal Child. We may lose conscious awareness of our child self, which becomes hidden beneath later experience-patterns, *but it is always there,* happy or unhappy, pleased or resentful, enthusiastic or discouraged, according to treatment received, and quite independently of the feelings of our outer self.

We don't easily perceive the child aspect in ourselves, nor in people of the same sex (or other grouping) as ourselves.

Thus Plato went, full of the new rationalist approach to philosophy, to the priests of Egypt (who with their animal-headed deities and less systematized thinking must have seemed to represent in some ways a less mature outlook on life), only to be told by them, "The Greeks are children." So likewise women easily see the child in men, and men see it in women. IN FACT, every person has some adult aspects and some child aspects, and these will vary in degree from time to time. Why not? — even the most sedate dog, cat or horse will break out occasionally for a youthful frolic.

So *respect* the child in your partner, as well as respecting the man or the woman: not with the "Men are just big children!" of the condescending female, nor with the "Women are so childish!" of the chauvinistic male, The man or the woman is a REAL man or woman, and the child in each one is a REAL child, without whose presence neither man nor woman would be a complete, understandable, likeable person. What would any of us be like without our hobbies, our relaxations, even our small vanities?

So in our relationship with one another, a sexual partnership does not and should not rule out other relationships with the same person; paradoxically the very sexuality which has separated us from the days of our childhood, now creates the charmed circle of that intimacy in which we can recapture the magick and the make-believe, the tenderness and the fun, of childhood.

In your intimate times together, you and your partner can build up a heightened appreciation of one another, and of your love-making, if you do not hurry on to directly sexual contacts. In touching and exploring each other's bodies, you will find there is much pleasure and understanding to be gained from handling, as well as from passively being handled. For this reason, although you should both indicate by sounds or signs what touches you find particularly enjoyable, you should, likewise, forbear to check caresses which do nothing for you; they may mean a lot to the partner who is giving them. A woman can enjoy passing her palms repeatedly over her man's shoulders; to some men this is a turn-on, but to others it means little. Unless the man finds it distracting or irritating, he should let her continue her enjoyment; he should try to imagine and appreciate her sensuous delight, for instance, in savoring the difference between his muscular flesh and her own.

A man may find deep emotional satisfaction as well as sexual stimulation in handling a woman's breasts; many women enjoy receiving this attention, but some don't. If it causes the woman positive irritation, discomfort or nausea she should of course indicate that the man should transfer his touching to another region of her body, but if she simply "gets nothing out of it" she should refrain from stopping him. If she relaxes and turns her imagination to sharing in her partner's pleasure and stimulation, she is likely to gain a good experience from it after all, and the totality of their lovemaking will certainly be improved by her acceptance.

The more complete body contact and appreciation there is, the less emphasis will be placed upon each partner's reaction to specific turn-ons; and in this way more tenderness and consideration *and real love* are likely to infuse the whole session.

When you touch, or think about, your partner's body or any part of it, cherish a feeling that *it's yours too.* (Encourage your partner to feel the same way about *your* body.) This applies to the sex organs just as to any other part, so that in your physical sharing you are together a complete composite being. The male organs belong to the woman as much as to the man, the female organs belong to the man as much as to the woman. Both of you can think of them as "ours".

That bodily joint-ownership is the basis of sexual partnership, and reinforces the Anima-Animus awareness in the psyche of each partner.

(The *mind* of each partner is a different matter. Both of you should beware of assuming you ought to be a pair of think-alikes. By all means rejoice in the feelings, ideas and views you have in common, but don't force it. That *isn't* what your love-sex relationship is about! Explore, understand, appreciate each other's individuality continually, for each person is a unique marvel; give help when wanted — dieting, stopping smoking and similar situations — but any move in the direction of a makeover or a takeover should be *banned*.)

Explore, caress, appreciate; welcome, savor, and enjoy desire, for desire is a friend and strengthener of love and *not* an enemy to be destroyed as soon as its presence is felt.

Not every love-session need end in sexual union.
Not every sexual union need end in ejaculation.

This book will have more on the topic, but here it leads on naturally to some discussion of two subjects which for some people can overshadow every consideration of physical love-making: the subjects of impotence and frigidity.

Sexual impotence, in the man, is generally understood as an inability either to obtain an erection or to maintain one long enough to achieve entry and/or emission. It can be a symptom of some condition needing medical or psychiatric attention; but most often it is a result of fatigue, stress or fear, or of massive self-medication meant to relieve those states. *Very frequently it is a result of worry or fear concerning sexual impotence, and is thus a self-fulfilling anxiety.*

In this connection it is most important to bear in mind that the erection of the penis results from a quite complex action of *involuntary nerves* and tissues. A man may be familiar with his own reactions, or a woman may be familiar with those of her partner, to an extent which makes an erection almost infallibly predictable in certain given conditions, but it is never as certain as, for instance, raising a finger at will.

If you plan to raise a finger and, at the attempt, nothing happens, there is indeed cause for concern, because your conscious mind ought to be in charge of it; but if you plan a penile erection and nothing happens, or if the erection lasts only for a short time or does not culminate in an emission when this is desired, any concern ought to be limited to discovering and removing the causes of the trouble. *The accident certainly ought not to terminate the love-making, even for that session.* Love and sexuality have many modes of expression other than erection and emission, and even the permanently impotent have kept women devoted year in and year out; whereas most failures of male sexuality are only temporary if taken lightly.

Tim and Cathy had just arrived at their honeymoon hotel. As they unpacked they began romping a little, and soon he was chasing her in a playful pursuit which would, he imagined, end up on the bed. Laughing and squealing, she dodged into the bathroom and, as he followed, without much thought she seized a bottle of liquid soap and sprayed him with it. He'd been laughing too, and the scented liquid caught him in the mouth.

It gave him something of a shock, and by the time he'd rinsed the taste away, the erection he had had was totally gone. Even when he pulled Cathy to him and kissed her, he could induce no response in his own body. As the evening passed, he began to be more and more worried about the wedding-night and proportionately less and less sociable to his bride.

Cathy was tired after all the excitement of the day, and despite some disappointment she was on the whole pleased to fall asleep after no more than a gentle embrace.

In the next two days, however, it became plain that Tim had some serious problem on his mind. Then, during the third night, matters reached a crisis. Perhaps he had a brief erection; anyway, he flung himself upon Cathy, hurt her and frightened her to no purpose, and, wailing "It's not going to be any good!" he left her, dressed himself, and spent the rest of the night chain-smoking in the lounge.

Next day Cathy returned to her folks and in due course she obtained an annulment. She and Tim never saw each other again. She never remarried, and it was many years before Tim in middle life met a handsome widow who gave him confidence enough to make another match. Through mutual friends Cathy heard of his new marriage and, since Tim hadn't explained to her a word of his problems, she was rather shocked that he had chosen such an experienced lady as her successor; all the same, she declared she herself would never love any man but he. He, too, always kept deep regrets about Cathy.

That was a tragedy of ignorance and of convention: Tim's youthful ignorance on how to deal with a temporary impotence — obviously it need only have been temporary — plus the convention that a man HAS TO produce an erection at will, and especially that a bridegroom HAS TO consumate his marriage at the first opportunity. It is not only a true story: there are frequent enough happenings of the same kind, or close to it, to make it important from the viewpoint of our subject.

What could Tim have done?

First, he needn't have made a calamity of it from the beginning. He and Cathy were secure in their own hotel room, the jokes and sly hints of their friends left far behind; they'd both had a tiring and exacting day, and, no matter how their imaginations might want them to celebrate their wedding night, their nervous systems had had enough. Tim's nervous system had taken a simple and obvious way to tell him so, but he hadn't wanted to heed it and as a result both his conscious and his unconscious mind had been thrown into complete panic.

He might have heeded the warning and realized that it doubtless applied to Cathy as well. He could have given her a lot of tenderness and affection, a lot of love and pride in their new partnership; and they could have fallen asleep happily in each others' arms. That way, Tim would have kept control of the situation, and Cathy would not have felt emotionally hurt and rejected as she soon came to do. Without doubt, since he didn't really mind the soap incident, they would have consummated their marriage within a day or so.

There is a technique which can be used with good effect *in the right circumstances* to cope with occasional impotence: for instance, if a single opportunity for intercourse has to be seized upon and maybe the very specialness of the occasion itself causes the man a sexual collapse. *If his partner is understanding and co-operative as well as physically habituated to intercourse, and if he himself can be patient and good-humored in the circumstances,* it is possible to manoeuver a semi-stiff or near-flaccid penis into the vagina. Once this is achieved, the partners should remain still for a few minutes; the probability being that the penis, like a certain type of actor, on finding itself "on stage" or "on location" will be restored suddenly to the full will and ability to perform. This is worth remembering for more experienced couples; obviously it could be of no use to a tense, worried young man and his virgin bride. In all cases, however, the chief factor for success in dealing with impotence is a realization that it isn't the end of the world!

It is not desirable, as we shall show, that a man should have an ejaculation at every embrace *even when he easily can.* Most emphatically, he should not attempt to drive himself in this respect when there is difficulty.

Female frigidity is a different problem as regards its usual causes, but the way to cope with it follows much the same lines. It *can* be a matter for a physician or therapist, but in most cases there is no treatment so effective as that of love, patience and tender reassurance. Non-sexual body contacts are of very great importance here. While a sexually robust woman may feel insulted if her man DOESN'T see her sometimes as a "sex symbol," the frigid woman needs constant emphasis on his reassurance that she is loved and cherished *as a person.*

There is however a special type of frigidity which has no psychological tie-ups, and which is due simply to lack of neural sensitivity. This is related to the very individual matter of the "pain threshold", and little can usually be done about it except by the woman herself. If she does not cultivate qualities of sympathy and imagination, such a woman can easily lead a detached and unemotional life, wondering merely what other people make so much fuss about. If however she has a warm and outgoing personality, she can be almost as much involved in the human drama as more sensitive types; in some ways, since she will be less demanding, she may well bring more happiness into the lives of those around her.

Sylvia J. was such a woman. Petite and slim, she might have seemed childlike or even boyish but for the blouson-type dresses, spike heels and sparkling jewelry she habitually wore. She chose perfumes carefully too. She'd had one happy marriage, with two children — a quiet, studious boy and a live-wire girl — but her husband Ken had been killed in a car accident, and now she was courting an attractive and rather younger man, Frank.

One holiday, Frank was out of town and Sylvia went for a country walk with a woman friend. They climbed a steep hill and sat down on the grass at the top, kicking off their shoes while they were getting their breath and enjoying the view.

While Sylvia was absorbed in identifying distant landmarks, her friend quietly plucked a fairly stiff grass-stem and drew it briskly from toe to heel of Sylvia's upturned sole. Not getting the expected jump and shriek of response, she was about to try again when Sylvia turned her head and said almost sadly, "You can do that as often as you like, it makes no difference to me!"

The friend paused, considering what this meant and remembering a couple more odd things: the time Sylvia had volunteered to cope with a hot skillet when there was no pot-holder, the way she'd gone into hospital each time a week before her babies had been expected, as if the usual signals couldn't be relied upon. She asked, *"Sylvia — are you like that all over?"*

Sylvia realized she'd given away her whole secret. "Yes," she replied. "But please don't tell anyone. Ken never knew, and if Frank found out it would spoil all his fun!"

Maybe Sylvia carried her sexy "act" further than was strictly necessary — "over-compensation" — but she provides an excellent instance of what is called "benevolent frigidity": a state in which a woman is unable, from whatever cause, to become sexually aroused but is favorable to, and does what she can to stimulate, arousal in her partner. Sylvia knew, too, one of the most important principles of the Magick of Sex. By showing physical pleasure, even though in her case it wasn't genuine, she did much towards her partner's enjoyment; and, too, although she could not enjoy sex physically, she found a lot of *emotional* pleasure in witnessing, imagining and sharing her partner's enjoyment. Thus she lived a happy, love-filled life.

No matter how rich in sexual feeling your own life may be, the same principles of patience, sympathy and sharing will apply in one way or another if your love-sex experience is to be all it can be. You can't run it all on instinct, any more than you can run it on intellect; you are a total human being and it is YOU with all the faculties and attributes of both your body and your psyche, who are needed in your role as a lover. You should take every opportunity to bestir and co-ordinate the various levels of your being, not simply one with another as in other types of inner activity, but here, above all, with those of your partner.

This is a relationship of body to body, instinct to instinct, emotion to emotion, and mind to mind; it can become a relationship of spirit to spirit. (In a certain sense, the relationship of spirit to spirit *is always there,* but that is a different kind of love and may take longer to realize.)

You need to get to know your partner in the ordinary way, as a person — even if you've been to- gether for years you may not have had too much time to do that — and to give your partner a chance to get to know you. Unless you are really determined about this, you may find you make no progress; even vacations can be as crowded-out with irrelevant comings and goings as are your working days. If you plan it properly, however, a vacation, a week-end or even a succession of evenings (summer or winter, with their different atmo- spheres and modes of intimacy) can be made into a true honeymoon of mutual discovery and appreciation at all levels.

The psycho-physical energizers we are about to give can be used in a variety of ways. They are in their essence preludes to sexual activity rather than being meant as sexual activity in themselves; but *all* actions between lovers are in a general sense sexual, and to draw any rules is neither possible nor to be wished. How IMMEDIATE a prelude to sex these techniques may be will depend upon the partners and upon the occasion.

Much depends, too, on how you perform them. If you were simply to go through the physical actions without adding any inner activity to them, probably even then you would both, or at least one of you would, be aware of really gaining something from them. But if you both perform the inner work, the visualizations, faithfully and to the best of your ability, you will certainly both gain a great deal from them; and what you gain will increase with practice, to the enhancement of your love-making and of both your lives.

DON'T BE AFRAID OF THE WORD "VISUAL-IZATION"! If you haven't encountered this kind of inner activity before, you may not understand what a very simple thing you are being asked to do.

It is simple, and natural, and easy.

It is, partly, a kind of make-believe which becomes real; but also, in the way we use it here, it is a kind of make-believe which *makes real for you,* and powerfully strengthens, *something which to some extent is there already.* That is the reason why we can say, even if you didn't visualize anything you might well be conscious to some extent of gaining something from these Energizers.

However, you want to gain all you can from them, so visualize!

Some people can visualize so vividly, they really

feel they are seeing what is described, either outside themselves as in physical seeing, or inside their head. Some other people's visualization does not "show" them anything, but gives them a strong certainty that what they have built up mentally is really present to them, and that by going along with the "image" they can direct and control it (which is true). Again, other people visualize in a way which is between these two extremes.

ALL THESE METHODS, OR ANY OTHER METHODS WHICH MAY COME TO YOU, ARE GOOD.

So don't think your visualization is a "failure" if you can't view your inner creations as on a television screen!

Another important point to remember is that it's *you* who have to do the visualizing. It is of no use for you merely to "switch on" inwardly and expect to watch a ready-made show. (If you can do that, it's not exactly the same thing. You may have kept a very vivid imagination from your childhood, in which case that faculty may be in danger of "running away" and showing you what *it* pleases instead of keeping to your intended visualization; or you may be clairvoyant, or you may have both clairvoyance and a vivid imagination. In any of these cases, you'll need to learn to "switch off" so that it's your conscious mind which controls the visualized image.)

So when we say "visualize," we mean, see inwardly if you can, or at least know mentally that what we describe is there; and keep the same visualization going until either it's time to change to a different image or you wish to let the image fade away. By visualizing in this way, you and your partner can really stimulate the movement of natural force corresponding to the image, and this will make your energization truly dynamic.

Where do these currents of force come from? As a living being you attract and absorb them, you fashion them and send them forth, knowingly or unknowingly. Energy never goes out of existence; you absorb it from the sunlight, the air, the rain, the earth, the food you eat — from innumerable sources — you can transmute it into action, you can give it forth as physical or emotional warmth, you can exchange it with other beings in countless ways. It flows through us and around us at every level of our existence. But also we can control and direct it in specific ways for specific purposes; the more practice we have, and the more we develop ourselves inwardly, the higher will be the levels at which we can direct it.

There is much more you can know about these currents, which can be directed for healing, for self-defense and many different uses; but in this particular book we are giving the simplest essentials, so you can use them in your own ways and find those paths to love-bliss which are most congenial for you and your partner.

Spiral Energizer

This is a powerful way to begin a love-session. Both partners should be unclothed and barefoot, and should stand facing each other, close but not touching.

(1) Each partner moves the right foot forward slightly, setting it down so that the heel rests on the ground while the toes rest gently but firmly upon the partner's left instep. Both partners should be able to stand quite steadily in this position, with the main weight of the body upon the left leg.

Standing thus, each partner, keeping the elbows at the sides, should raise the hands to a level between breast and shoulder, fingers extended upwards, palms forwards, so that the palm of each hand is pressed gently against the palm of the partner's opposite hand.

(2) Maintaining this position, with no parts of their bodies touching except the feet and hands, both partners should visualize a stream of white light ascending from ground level, flashing as it coils around the two of them in an anti-clockwise spiral. More of this light continually comes up, spiraling around the couple and disappearing overhead, so that they are enclosed in endless ascending spiral streams of flashing white light.

The partners should enjoy the experience of this light. They can do so in silence if they wish, or they can talk about it; if talking does not disturb their visualization, they will probably find describing it to each other will increase their awareness of the experience. They are being bathed in a swirling current of cool, energizing white light which rises all about them, and they can stand thus for as long as they wish before going on to the next stage. (They can let each other know of their readiness to move on, either by speech or by a signal.)

(3) Having allowed the previous visulaization to fade from consciousness, the partners draw back their right feet and place them alongside the left, so each person stands normally. Each partner now places the palm of his or her left hand upon the forehead of the other, as nearly as possible with the center of the palm upon the center of the brow, and extends his or her right hand to the other's genitals. The way in which this is done should be intimate and erotic without any violence or urgency of movement. The woman may cup with her hand the genitals of the man, the man may put his palm to the woman's genitals, placing the tip of his middle finger at the opening of her vagina — or other positions of the right hands upon the genitals can be chosen as the couple may desire — but when once the position is taken up there should be little or no movement and only gentle pressure.

(4) Maintaining this position, with no bodily contact other than that just described, both partners should visualize a stream of white light descending from overhead, flashing as it coils around the two of them in an anti-clockwise spiral. More of this light continually descends, spiraling around the couple and disappearing at their feet, so that they are bathed in endless descending spirals of flashing, energizing white light.

As before, the partners may share this experience either in silence or with words. Their visualization should not only be directed to an inner faculty of "sight"; they should seek to *feel* imaginatively the impulses of energy which pass through them as the light swirls and flashes; at the same time, they should relax by an effort of will any tenseness which may begin to build up in their bodies as a result of this energization or of the hand-contact. *The more relaxation and passivity they can maintain while receiving this stage of the energization, the greater will be the effect in their subsequent love-making.*

This visualization therefore should be kept up for at least as long as the previous one, and should not be shortened through impatience; but when the partners have experienced it sufficiently, they should by agreement pass on to the next stage.

(5) Having allowed the previous visualization to fade from consciousness, the partners move closer together, with body surfaces in contact but in other particulars returning to the posture described in (1) above: each places the right foot so the toes rest on the other's left instep, with hands palm to palm.

They bring their mouths together in a kiss, as prolonged and passionate as desired. (The hands, at first kept palm to palm, in the course of this kiss move naturally into an embrace.)

(6) While kissing, the partners should visualize a stream of *rose-colored* light ascending from ground

level, flashing with brilliant bursts of the same color as it coils around the two of them in an anti-clockwise spiral. More of this light rises continually, spiraling around the couple and disappearing overhead, so that they are bathed in endless ascending spiral streams of rose-colored, warmly energizing light.

The partners should not neglect this visualization; no matter how passionate their embrace, they should feel themselves to be passively receptive meanwhile to the impulses of energy which surge through them as the glowing light swirls and flashes, heightening their vitality and linking them ever more closely to one another.

They can stand thus for as long as they wish; then, letting the visualization fade from awareness, they may proceed as pleases them.

Palm-to-Palm Energizer

The position of the hands given in section (1) of the Spiral Energizer is, in itself, a valuable energization and harmonizing technique for man and woman. It can be employed when fully clothed, and in any situation where a few minutes' privacy is possible. *No visualization is needed.*

The palm-to-palm energizer is a good preliminary for love-making, especially where harmony, staying power and mutual support are seen as the main requirements. It is, however, also excellent before (or in the course of) any other activity in which the couple engages:

a session of dancing or of physical exercise, a tennis game or even a card-party. Simply stand facing each other close but not touching, raise your hands and press them gently palm-to-palm, as described, for a few minutes.

Let your gaze and your partner's meet meanwhile.

You can expect a resulting refreshment to the nervous system, an increased rapport between your partner and yourself, and an exchange and balancing of male/female polarities; all benefiting the physical and mental powers of both partners.

Feet-to-Feet Energizer

This, like the preceding, makes an excellent preparation for a couple to use before a love-session or before other activities where it is desired to enhance co-ordination between the partners as well as the inner co-ordination of each one. It is less possible than the palm-to-palm energizer to "do anywhere", but it allows a greater degree of relaxation and thus of direction to a purpose.

Visualization can be used if desired.

The partners may be clothed or unclothed, but any tight belts or garments should be loosened. Shoes should be removed; light hosiery is optional.

(1) The partners lie down on their backs in an adequate floor-space, legs together, heads pointing in opposite directions, the feet of one partner sole-to-sole with the feet of the other. Some adjustment of position may be needed so both can lie with legs straight but

Spiral Energizer

not stretched, feet touching at both heel and toe but not pressed forcibly against each other.

Arms should lie naturally at the sides; the face should be directed upwards, but with the chin slightly lowered for comfort. Eyes should be closed.

The partners should remain thus, maintaining a firm but gentle contact with the feet, while relaxing and being aware of each other's sustaining presence. They may also reflect, but without anxiety, upon the intended activity which is to follow this Energizer.

Suitably peaceful music meanwhile is helpful.

(2) *(Optional)* While lying in this state of relaxation, each partner visualizes, or develops awareness of, a circulation of energy in the form of a stream of sparkling white light which runs continuously from the sole of the left foot, up the left leg, side and arm to the head, down the right side and arm and down the right leg to the sole of the right foot.

(More important than "seeing" is to "feel" in imagination this continuous stream of energy as it flows vibrant, shimmering and flashing, mentally directed in its rapid course. Each person should concentrate only on being aware of, and guiding, the unpausing current as it flows around his or her own body from left foot to right foot. *In fact, however,* a complete circuit of shared power is formed encompassing the two partners, its flow being channeled by the alternate polarities of their feet: the right feet, giving, juxtaposed with the left feet, receiving.

On an agreed signal to end the practice, both partners should allow the visualization to fade gently. They should lie peacefully for at least a half minute more before bringing the muscles back from their relaxed state and preparing to resume other activity.

The next energizer resembles the Spiral Energizer notably by culminating in a kiss, and also has some other features in common with that technique.

Kissing is of great importance in the Magick of Sex, and in the mysticism of sex. It is important primarily because of its power of arousal at both the physical and the imaginative levels of the personality, as an activating key to symbolisms rooted deeply in the lower unconscious levels of the psyche. But that is not all. It is important also because of its potent significance in the eroto-mystical symbolisms of the higher unconscious, of which more will be said later in this book; the kiss has been taken by profoundly mystical authorities to represent experiences which can be represented only by likeness.

Intoxicating kisses, sense-ravishing kisses, kisses which raise delight to a pitch where personal identity loses itself: these are recognized by our inner being as a token, even a foretaste, of that touch of the Divine which raises humanity to its own level.

Sweet Helen, make me immortal with a kiss! –

Her lips suck forth my soul; see where it flies –
cries Marlowe's Faustus to, and of, the mythic Lady of Troy, in a drama which is filled with medieval and

Renaissance learning on hidden matters.

This energizer is a variant of the traditional Qabalistic technique for intensifying the operation of the *Centers of Activity* or "chakras". Since we exist in various dimensions simultaneously — spiritual, mental, astral and material — it is essential to our effectiveness as living beings that we should encourage the inter-communication of those levels. The Centers of Activity hold a unique place in this process, for although they exist primarily at the subtle level of the astral body they have also a correspondence to the different dimensions of the psyche. They are truly the great gateways by and through which the life-force is channeled, and are the principal instruments of its organization and direction. Thus their balanced activation can, and should, induce equilibrium and vitality at all levels.*

The standard Qabalistic procedure is to activate the Centers *from the top downwards,* initiating a descent of power from the spiritual source at the outset. In this special formulation of the practice for the Magick of Sex, however, the Centers are activated in reverse, in ascending order. Thus, by implication, all that the partners are, and have, and hold, is raised by degrees from the mundane to the celestial; is carried to ever higher and more inward levels of shared experience. Finally, the descent of power is initiated, linking all the levels in its downward course.

*More concerning the principal Centers and their activation can be found in Volume IV of *The Magical Philosophy* (Llewellyn, St. Paul) pages 113 through 116 and 247 through 250.

Central Column Energizer

This is a complex energizer, and its various parts should be given careful attention until the whole can be harmoniously practiced. It has great power and beauty, and will amply repay thorough mastery.

It is recommended that the partners learn to perform it throughout with closed eyes. They can, where appropriate, and to assist their unified awareness, speak while establishing a shared visualization; for changes of posture and the beginning and end of visualization, the partners should arrange and practice with one another beforehand suitable touch-signals, such as by finger pressure. They should, in this, create a system which is agreeable to themselves.

For the purpose of this energizer, in which the partners are very close together, each Center is visualized as shared, one Center between the two, and as a sphere of about five inches across.

The partners are unclothed, and barefoot. They

Central Column Energizer — Position of Feet

stand facing each other, close together but at first not touching each other, arms at the sides.

1.   Both partners take a step forward so that each one's feet form (roughly) a right angle between them, and the four feet together form a square (again roughly). They join hands loosely, right hand over left at each side.

This position allows a contact of bodies if the partners lean somewhat forward; they should be able to do this without losing balance.

2.   Standing thus, the partners visualize, faintly luminous about their feet, a sphere of pearly-grey light which is half above floor level, half below. In it are gleams of pale lemon yellow, olive green, russet and black.*

Having realized the sphere and its colors as clearly as possible, the partners contemplate it for a while; then, maintaining the posture, they allow the visualization to fade from consciousness.

3.   Each partner now places his or her hands on the hips of the other, drawing the pelvic region closer so that the genitals touch.

4.   As the contact is established, the partners visualize, centered in the genitals, a sphere of violet-colored light, brighter than the previous visualization.

---

* The sequence of colors employed in this energizer is not an arbitrary choice, but is derived from a Qabalistic system. It is a tested code which the deeper levels of the psyche will assimilate, so that those of its natural powers with which we are concerned will be stimulated and stabilized. For further information on the Qabalistic use of color, see Volume III of *The Magical Philosophy* (Llewellyn, St. Paul) pages 83 through 195.

This color should be as nearly as possible a perfect balance between blue and red, lustrous and beautiful. It should be contemplated by the partners, taking time for deep enjoyment both of the physical contact and of the visualized color. Then, maintaining the posture, they allow the visualization to fade from consciousness.

5. Each partner now places his or her hands on the shoulders of the other, and draws the upper torso forwards so that besides the genitals, the heart-regions of the partners now make contact, pressing gently against each other.

6. As this contact is established, the partners visualize, centered at the new point of contact, a sphere of clear yellow light, brighter than the previous visualizations and pulsating with the beating of their hearts. They remain awhile thus, rejoicing alike in the splendor of the light which belongs to them both and in the contact which is associated with it. Then, while still maintaining the posture, they allow the visualization to fade from consciousness.

7. Each partner now places his or her hands with the palms to the back of the other's neck, fingers interlocking. Each partner bends his or her own head back and somewhat to the left, against the supporting hands. They bring their throats as closely together as they can.

8. While in that posture, they visualize, centered between their throats, a sphere of very deep purple. The color is velvety and intense, with no gleam or suggestion of light or of any other color in it. The

partners should make it as perfect as they can, and should keep this visualization long enough to feel something of its deep peace and magnetism, but not as long as the previous visualizations before allowing it to fade from consciousness.

Still keeping feet, genitals and heart-regions in light contact, they bring their heads back to the normal position.

9.   Each partner now places his or her hands at the sides of the other's head, somewhat above and behind the ears, and draws the head forward. Then their mouths meet in a long and intense kiss.

10.   While they are kissing, they each visualize a sphere of light centered at the midpoint between their foreheads, *but in this instance they do not both visualize the same colors.* The man visualizes this sphere as indigo, deep and mysterious; the woman visualizes it as a dynamic nacreous vortex of all the spectrum colors. They give this experience sufficient time, then let the visualization fade.

11.   Without changing the position of their feet, they move their bodies slightly back from each other, and join hands to stand as in Section 1.

12.   While they stand thus, they visualize over-head a single sphere of intense white brilliance. When this is clearly established, they visualize a sudden ray of white descending from the sphere, vertically down to the ground between them. After a moment's contem-plation, the partners allow the whole visualization to fade.

This, and all the Psychic Energizers given in this chapter, will be found to have great power for use in different circumstances. Various occasions for the use of one or another energizer are indicated in the course of this book; when you are proficient in performing them you will find many more occasions in your own life.

You and your partner should practice them as much as possible, and should gain some proficiency even before putting the next chapter to practical use. Proficiency, however, will go on increasing with practice; you have here a valuable instrument for integrating and balancing your energies, individually and as a couple, at every level.

Checkpoint
2

- *Body Language* goes on communicating all the time, especially between yourself and your partner, whether consciously interpreted or not. This gives you two main points for care:

  (a) You and your partner need to make different aspects of yourselves interesting, appealing and intelligible to each other. The drama of play situations is valuable here.

  (b) Use normal verbal communication too, to make sure your partner gets the right interpretation of some perhaps negative signal you know you may be giving. If your partner is left to draw conclusions, the result may be a misunderstanding and hurt feelings.

- Remember there's a child hidden in every adult; but that only makes the adult more of a complete person!

● Sexuality comprises a lot more than just "having sex." You and your partner can build up your whole relationship into something vibrantly sexual, and much of this can be achieved by means of *minor bodily contacts* and *maintained physical appeal.*

● Broadening, in this way, the basis of sexuality in your lives should at once cut down to size the specters of impotence and frigidity which ruin the love-life of a lot of people!

(a) Male impotence often begins as a temporary problem resulting from fatigue, stress or anxiety, or from self-medication intended to relieve those states. It's essential to remove the cause: *anxiety about impotence itself is as bad a hazard as any,* and the woman can help here.

(b) Female frigidity often has psychological causes, *and here the man needs to help.* His partner is likely to need plenty of affection and appreciation; then her unconscious mind can begin to respond to sex as an authentic expression of love.

(c) Even where impotence and frigidity have unalterable physical causes, this isn't the end of love-life for a man or a woman who can focus attention on, and imaginatively enter into, the partner's emotions and physical pleasure.

• Even if you and your partner have been together for years, you may still find areas where you don't know each other. *Discover and explore! —* make yours a relationship of body to body, instinct to instinct, emotion to emotion and mind to mind. Be aware, too, that it's also a relationship of spirit to spirit.

• Practice with your partner the four Psychic Energizers: The Spiral, the Palm-to-palm, the Feet-to-feet, and the Central Column Energizer.

• Use one or other of the Psychic Energizers:
  (a) In relation to specific procedures and play situations, as given in this book.
  (b) Before sex, before a business meeting, before sport or any stressful activity.
  (c) By themselves, whether for practice, to help one or both of you "unwind" or combat exhaustion, or just as something good to do together.

N. B. These are guide-lines, *not rules,* for using the Psychic Energizers. Use them spontaneously whenever you feel they are "right."

Study Points
3

1. Erotic Massage has more than physical benefit for the person receiving it: it involves the use of psychic energy to not only heighten pleasure but also to intensify the actual unity of the partners.

2. An additional advantage to Erotic Massage is the purely physical value in toning and relaxing the body, extending awareness to the entire body, increasing our respect for and appreciation of bodily health and condition, and in increasing knowledge and understanding of each other's bodies.

3. Erotic Massage also offers a basic opportunity for role exchanges: each partner at different times being active or passive. For many people this switch in interactive dynamics is ordinarily difficult, so

conditioned are we to traditional patterns. This exchange sets a pattern for removing internal psychic barriers inhibiting the free flow of energy and functioning of various components that make up the psyche.

4. In addition to the technique of massage taught here, there is the *Charging Breath* — a psychic technique for focusing *Odic Energy* on certain points of the body, and by its means projecting emotion and purpose. This is a highly effective and very magical technique traditional to the Western Mysteries.

5. You will need a nice scented massage lubricant, towels, and comfortable massage table or pad or firm mattress — and little else to open yourselves to a wonderful way of multi-level communication and stimulation that will find many values in your lives.

3

Erotic Massage

The massage technique given in this chapter is not meant only for the physical benefit of the person who receives it. It is an erotic massage, and includes the use of psychic energy; it will not only heighten pleasure, but should intensify for both partners their awareness of unity in feeling and experience.

There are fashions in the popular term for massage. Once "rubbing" was popular, now gentler terms such as "stroking" are preferred. In reality neither of these terms gives an adequate description of what is needed; and most types of massage employ a variety of movements from which the user either selects according to previous training, or makes a spontaneous choice which has regard to the part of the body being massaged and the effect desired.

Here we employ three explicit movements, and a fourth which is more general.

1.   *Stroking* — firmly with the fingers alone, or, quite

often, strongly with the whole palmar surface of the hand, and in some cases with the heel of the hand. Used for example from the extremities towards the trunk in relaxing arms and legs, or working on distended veins or lymphatic stagnation (puffy ankles due to tiredness or prolonged standing).

2.   *Kneading* — with the thumbs, the heel of the hand and/or the knuckles, as when dealing with a large area of stiffness in the back muscles following over-exercise, for instance, or with a heavy deposit of fat on the abdomen. (You can't "cure" fatness in this way, but by increasing the circulation you help the removal of waste products from the clogged tissues, and give your partner a good, "toned" feeling which encourages perseverance in a diet or so forth.) Kneading the abdomen deeply with the knuckles, proceeding in a clockwise direction, is also a good toner but should be avoided if it causes any pain.

3.   *Tapping* — This is a gentler method, which can therefore be more prolonged, to stimulate circulation in stiff or fatty areas; it can also be used quite firmly as a toner for the spinal column. Gentle tapping is used where it's desirable to massage and stimulate but most undesirable to risk even slightly stretching the skin: for instance, when working around a recently-healed scar, or, in facial massage, on the cheeks just below the eyes.

4.   *"Handling"* — Done chiefly with the fingers, and in a variety of ways. The toes, for instance, can be "picked up" one at a time, rolled and squeezed (but

not pinched), pulled and stimulated. The ears are more significant in erotic massage than in most other techniques: they too are "handled", being gently pulled back and forth, but also having the lobe and the shell enjoyably pinched. In erotic massage, naturally, "handling" also describes the various movements applied to the genitals.

In the type of psycho-physical massage we are considering here, moderate but firm movements of the hands all over the body, varying in type according to the area being massaged, are the most suitable.

BEWARE OF CAUSING PAIN!

You may have heard how an osteopath for example, or a Rolfer, will sometimes cause a person a great deal of temporary pain, with entirely and lastingly good results.

That is no example for you to follow!

Those practitioners are highly trained people who know exactly what to do, and how and when to do it. Without such knowledge, the only safe course is the plain and natural one: *Pain is a warning signal, and we should* stop at once *whatever causes it.*

Of course, if you have blundered upon a nerve-spot in your partner's shoulder, elbow or knee, and he or she expresses pain, you need *only* stop, and avoid that spot for the future. But if you find you cause pain by doing something you'd reasonably expect to be painless (like stroking the breast, kneading the abdomen, or straightening a toe) then to have the opinion of a physician as to the cause of it would be a good idea. That's one of the ways mutual massage can help you and your partner in understanding your own and each other's bodies; if any little thing should be amiss, it can be noticed and dealt with more promptly than might otherwise be the case.

There are, however, more benefits in home massage than obvious physical ones. It is a way in which the partners can alternate loving, giving action when performing the massage, with trusting, receptive passivity when enjoying it. It is a way in which they can learn to awaken and to experience delight in every part of the body, discovering the considerable pleasure which can be felt in even their least erogenous areas. Thus it can open up a whole new dimension in the partners' emotional relationship with one another.

Conversation during massage is undesirable. Certainly the recipient of the massage is entitled to say if he or she is hurting, or would like a rest, or anything of that sort; while the giver of the massage likewise — especially during the first few sessions — may need to say something like "Am I pressing too hard?" or "I must rest my arms for a minute now!" But these occasions should be kept to a minimum, and in all likelihood will virtually disappear when both partners have a little more practice and experience in massage.

(In any case, if either partner calls for a rest, hand

contact should be maintained during the interval so that the psychic continuity of the massage is not broken.)

Talking distracts from the physical and psychic rapport in which the partners should become absorbed during massage: if it leads to the expression of random thoughts, it can break that rapport altogether. Furthermore, research has shown that conversation with *any human being,* no matter what the topic, always raises the blood-pressure to some extent, and even the slightest degree of this is to be avoided if possible while giving or receiving massage.

If you and your partner decide massage is to be a regular feature of your intimate life, you should invest in a portable massage table. This is much better than any other arrangement for the purpose.

The next best thing is a firm mattress or a well-padded exercise mat placed on a sturdy kitchen or office table. The whole should be about 30 inches high, more or less: low enough for you to be able to exert firm pressure, high enough to avoid tiring your back in leaning forward to do so.

Whatever you choose, cover the surface with towels or something similar so you don't need to worry about oil spots. Have other cloths ready too, to wipe away surplus oil from your hands or your partner's skin if it becomes uncomfortable; you may also find a similarly covered pillow is a good thing, to place under the knees of the person being massaged when he or she is lying face upwards, aiding relaxation by steadying the legs and feet. (Any pillow or pad placed under the head should be the thinnest that will be found effective.)

Apart from these things, the chief other require-ment will be a massage lubricant. This can be either a commercially-produced cream (expensive and usually more complex than is necessary) or a home-prepared oil (economical both in initial cost and in spreading-power, and completely effective for its purpose).

NEVER attempt to give the least amount of massage without lubrication of some kind.

Castor oil is excellent for the skin, but is somewhat heavy in use, has a peculiar smell, and can cause smarting if it gets in the eyes. It is also rather unpopular with women because it has a reputation, whether deservedly or not, for encouraging the growth of body hair. If used, it should be in a 50-50 mixture with a lighter type of oil such as that of cottonseed or sunflower.

Olive oil is a magnificent massage oil — in its crude form it was the favorite skin lubricant and skin nutrient of the almost fanatical body-culturists of classical Greece — and has an attractive natural fragrance, but may be found rather expensive. Again, dilution with sunflower or cottonseed oil, or *refined* corn oil, may be the answer.

Modern vegetable *cooking oils*, provided they have no chemical additives and, preferably, no strong culinary smell, can be used without mixing with any other oil if desired.

Lanolin (wool fat) is an emollient with which the skin has a certain natural affinity, and has been found especially useful for occasional use on dry or sensitive skin. In its pure form it is too stiff and heavy for use in massage, and would pull the skin badly. *Hydrous lanolin* is a pharmaceutical preparation of lanolin, combined with water to make it softer, more easily absorbed by the skin, and more suitable for massage. It is not customarily given routine use, but is employed for an occasional massage of face, neck and arms.

Whatever lubricant is chosen, it can be given an attractive smell by blending into it a small quantity of fragrant essence such as rose oil, or oil of jasmine, sandalwood or patchouli. Some health-food stores supply a variety of these essences in little phials; be sure, however, to choose an *oil*, not an alcohol-based essence, and one which is agreeable to both you and your partner and to which neither of you is allergic.

In erotic massage particularly, you should take care to *avoid giving shocks.* Physical stimulation is fine: shocks, whether physical or emotional (and usually they are both) are entirely negative and are a quick sexual turn-OFF. When we first come to using the massage oil, there will be a note on taking the chill off it in your hand before applying it to your partner's body; but further care is needed with the way you move:

a. When a deep heavy pressure is needed, as in a few instances using thumbs or knuckles, *never prod or punch.* Put the thumb or fist GENTLY on the place, then STEADILY intensify the pressure.

b. If a new set of movements sets you working on a different part of your partner's body from where you have been — if you have been standing at the feet for instance and the new movements begin at the fingers, or you move from thighs to upper abdomen — *don't suddenly manifest in the new area!* While you are moving you can place first one hand and then the other on your partner's body to make him or her aware of your change of position. Your partner may be dozing even without realizing it, or may be in a state of consciousness somewhat removed from full wakeful awareness; and being unclothed gives most of us a deep-level sense of vulnerability. A firm hand suddenly placed on the stomach or on the back of the neck can cause an unpleasant jolt, and undo a lot of your good work. So — signal where you are!

There's one more thing to know before beginning the massage: an easy way to transfer psychic energy to specific parts of the body. This is the *Charging Breath,* a traditional technique of the Western Mysteries which has many uses besides its application to the human body.

When it is applied to the body, most of the points on which it is usually focused are "pressure points"; and of these, many have a direct or indirect sexual relevance. Our massage uses some of the chief of these points; the Charging Breath provides an eminently simple, yet powerful and deep-reaching, mode of stimulating their subtle levels.

Breath carries *odic energy,* which is produced by the life-forces of the person who breathes it out. It has, besides, the character of its movement and impact. You can infuse your breath with your emotion and purpose; if you do this deliberately it becomes a potent instrument.

The mode of performing the Charging Breath in the course of massage is as follows:

With your mouth closed, take in through your nostrils a deep, steady breath. Hold it for a moment, then open your mouth over — *near but not touching — the area which is to receive the charge. With the purpose of conveying warmth, vitality and love to your partner, breathe out steadily and completely. This breathing, in and out, may be repeated several times over the same spot.*

Besides stimulating specific points, use of the Charging Breath intensifies that sexual attunement of one partner to the other which is produced by erotic massage. If the partners systematically massage each other, this sexual attunement will be progressive. However, since they may not on all occasions decide to complete the massage, there is the more reason to perform it OFTEN.

They may decide to perform the massage on special occasions, such as before a simple love-sex session, before a "play" session such as those suggested in

Chapters 4 and 5, before a "no-sex" session such as some of those suggested in Chapter 7, before Cosmic Awareness Intercourse as given in Chapter 8, or before the Rituals given in Chapter 9.

These possibilities indicate four distinct ways in which this Erotic Massage procedure can be used:

(i) Not completing the massage, letting it develop from any chosen point into a sex session.

(ii) Completing the massage, performing the Central Column Energizer at the end, then going on into a dynamic sexual experience.

(iii) Completing the massage and NOT having sex, for the joy of building up unfulfilled desire, with the heightened mutual love and awareness to be gained therefrom (See Chapter 7).

(iv) Completing the massage and going on, after using a psychic energizer if desired, to a ritual activity or a play situation.

EROTIC MASSAGE
(Psycho-physical Stimulation)

All having been made ready, it remains for the partners to prepare themselves.

A bath or shower is in order immediately before the massage, for both parties. The recipient will need to be unclothed during the massage; if the temperature is really low it may be desireable to cover parts of the body while they are not being actively worked on. Massage is, however, a great warmer-up for both giver and recipient, so unless the latter is in a poor state of health the need for cover is usually less than might appear. The giver of the massage may also be unclothed while in action, or should wear simple loose-fitting garments, and should be barefoot.

(1) Standing side by side and linking hands, you and your partner perform gentle and natural *deep breathing* for from two to five minutes. This should be done either in the open air or in the freshest air available, and with the least clothing which is convenient and comfortable.

(2) In the place where the massage is to take place, you and your partner stand facing each other and perform the Palm-to-Palm Energizer.

(3) Your partner now lies down, unclothed, face upwards, and takes about three really deep breaths in succession to ensure that the spine is straight. After making any necessary adjustment, he or she relaxes as much as is possible at this time. (It is natural and desirable that the state of relaxation should increase progressively during the course of the massage.) If desired, a pillow can be placed under the knees to aid relaxation of legs and feet, while the recipient is lying face upwards.

(4) Take a little oil in one hand, wait until it no longer feels cold to you, then spread it over your palms and fingers. (You should take oil in this same way, whenever more is needed. *Avoid Shock!)*

(5) Cupping the heel of one of the feet in your less active hand, with the thumb and forefinger of your other hand squeeze, roll, pull gently and move around in a circle each toe in turn, beginning with the little toe. (Toes of the right foot should be circled clockwise, toes of the left foot anti-clockwise.) When dealing with the big toe, your supporting hand should be moved up to grasp the instep, and the toe while being circled can be enclosed firmly in all the fingers of your working hand. If your partner has a problem with the toe joint, this joint can be given a gentle contouring massage, starting from the apex of the joint and moving in circles down it, provided it is not at all painful.

Repeat all the movements of this Section (5) on the other foot.

(6) Now, returning to the first foot, grasp the foot firmly in your two hands (fingers above, thumbs on the sole) and, using a firm stroking movement or a series of "taps," take your two thumbs strongly from the little-toe side to the big-toe side. Do this first on the ball of the foot just below the toes, then repeat, working across the foot in lines which move progressively down to the heel.

If you tap, you should alternate the movements of your thumbs, raising one while you lower the other. *Whatever movement you use, remember you want the effect, here, to reach deep below the surface.*

When you have gone over the complete sole, make the same movements in one vertical line from the tip of the big toe to the point of the heel; then place one hand under the sole of the foot, and with your other hand stroke the top of the foot firmly and rapidly several times from toes to instep.

Repeat all the movements of this Section (6) on the other foot.

(7) Perform the Charging Breath on the soles of your partner's feet, the focal point being the center of the arch of each foot.

(8) Have your partner turn over to lie face downwards, head turned to whichever side is comfortable. Relaxation should be renewed, as deeply as is possible.

(9) Beginning with the fingers, work up each arm in turn to the shoulder, using stroking and gentle squeezing movements: smooth veins *upwards* with your palm. (Keep clear of the "funny bone" and its special nerve in the elbow.) Make your movements rhythmic, steady and caressing, as if you were using them to hypnotize your partner; when you reach the shoulder in each case, work on it a little, making your movements more and more gentle, then ceasing.

(10) Beginning at the toes — which this time need, each, just a loving squeeze — work up each leg in turn to the buttock, using similar movements as for the arms but more strongly. Again, set up and keep a steady rhythm. Here the knee is the region for caution, both at the front and at the back: you can *gently* smooth upwards the veins at the back of the knee with the outer edges of your palms, but avoid any digging into that area.

(11) Beginning at the large bump in the spine at the base of the neck, handle and knead the muscles of the shoulders, back, waist and lumbar region. Caress with loving strength here. On the buttocks, use kneading and tapping movements at first; stroking follows and is maintained for a while, caressingly moving along the natural contours.

(12) Beginning again at the base of the neck, work down the spine, close to the backbone on both sides, with sharp tapping movements; you can use the tips of all your fingers bunched together, raising one hand as you lower the other. When you come to a point immediately below the lowest pair of ribs, press in firmly at each side of the spine with your thumbs; also perform the Charging Breath on the spine itself at this point. The aim is to stimulate some deep nerve centers in this region.

When you have continued tapping down to the base of the spine, place the heel of your hand on the tailbone, and press *strongly* several times; then use the Charging Breath on the tailbone.

(13) With sharp tapping movements work *up* the spine to the base of the neck, this time tapping on the vertebrae themselves.

(13A) *Man massaging Woman:* Besides the foregoing, when you reach the waistline, apply the knuckles of one hand *gently* to the spine at that point; press down slowly and strongly several times. Follow this with the Charging Breath focused on the same area: a warm and loving summoning of her inner response to you.

(14) Have *little* oil on your hands to massage your partner's head. Work (a) strongly up from the hairline to the crown with your fingers, starting from various points around the scalp and continually moving the scalp to and fro to loosen it; and (b) move gently down from the hairline to the base of the neck, handling and loosening the muscles. If the scalp is tight, give it more massage: this helps release tensions which are enemies of sexuality. Lovingly handle and pull the ears, manipulate them this way and that.

(14A) *Man massaging Woman:* Besides the above, caress the shells of the ears, hold them between thumb and finger and lift with gentle firmness towards the top of the head. Then gently bend each one in turn forward, and perform the Charging Breath focusing into the crevice behind it.

(15) Have your partner lie face upwards once more. Relaxation should be made as deep as possible. Stand behind your partner's head, cradle the head in your two hands, your fingers at the sides of the neck. Remain thus, motionless, for some minutes to aid relaxation.

(16) Beginning with the fingers, work up each arm in turn to the shoulder with stroking, caressing movements, and give particular attention to handling and loosening the big muscles which run from the shoulder joints upwards to the sides of the neck. As before, however, avoid exerting strong movement on the neck itself.

(16A) *Woman massaging Man:* When beginning the foregoing, give extra time to massaging the wrists; circle with your thumb on the back of each wrist, and also perform the Charging Breath upon those same places. You can send psychic thrills through him with this!

(17) Squeeze and pull each toe in turn, with particular attention and special stroking for the little toe on each foot. Then, facing the soles of the feet, grasp one foot with both your hands, fingers over the instep. Press your two thumbs firmly into the arch of the foot and stroke strongly and rhythmically, over and over, towards the heel, as if you meant to lift the bones of the arch. Although this is a strong movement, it should be pleasurable and soothing. Use plenty of oil and give enough time to each foot.

(17A) *Woman massaging Man:* Besides the foregoing, pay attention to the area between the ankle-bone and the heel tendon on the inner side of each foot. It is a pressure-point relating to penile erection, so give it your loving care: a circling pressure with your thumb, and a Charging Breath focused into the center of this area.

(18) Stroke each leg with long, rhythmic movements all round it; on the front of the leg, stroke firmly up to the groin. Parting the legs, use the Charging Breath on a number of areas on the inner side of each thigh — you'll not find a non-responsive point.

(19) Tap strongly on the pit of the stomach (the triangle just below the ribs.) Then press into this area

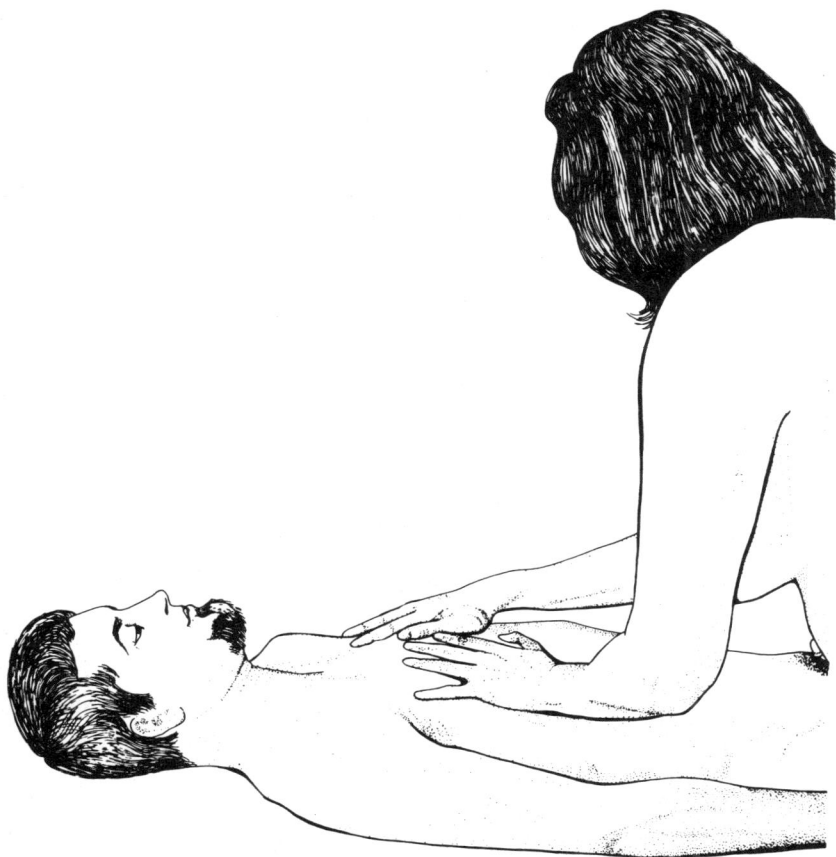

Joanne Cook Westbrook

gently but stongly with the knuckles of one hand, using a slight circling movement. Repeat this several times; your partner should try to relax the muscles while you do it. Use the Charging Breath here: the nerves of the stomach often need help to free themselves from stress.

(20) First tapping, then kneading, move your hands in *clockwise* circlings over the entire abdomen; gently at first, then more firmly and deeply, finally kneading as strongly as you can without causing pain. (By aiding intestinal action, this helps sexuality and general well-being).

(21) Contour the breasts with gentle, rhythmic stroking. Use the Charging Breath on the nipples, then proceed here as you and your partner may desire.

(21A) *Man massaging Woman:* Before contouring breasts, tap firmly down center-line of breastbone from collar-bones to pit of stomach, several times. This reverberates an important glandular center.

(22) Use firm tapping movements with the four fingers of each hand (as on spine) down the center line of the abdomen from the pit of the stomach to the genital region. This is an effective sexual toner.

(23) Perform the Charging Breath on the genitals; then proceed with gentle stroking around the outer boundary of the genital organs to the perineum (that is the muscular bridge between the back of the sex organs and the anus). With one thumb, or with one of your forefingers pressing on the other forefinger, press firmly into *the middle* of the perineum. Although as

will be shown in a later chapter, this pressure can inhibit immediate ejaculation for a man, it is in other circumstances a sexual arouser for either man or woman.

(23A) *Woman massaging Man:* If you can be both firm and gentle at the same time, the most exhilarating final touch you can give this massage is to take up, handle, and then give a squeeze to, the testicles. *Squeeze, not pinch!* — if you make a mistake you may never get another chance!

The above is the outline of a massage procedure which can be thoroughly helpful and renewing, physically and psychically, while incorporating some powerful erotic boosters. As given, it is geared for active folk who often need to free themselves from the stresses of their workaday world before being able to put their best into love-making.

If you are skilled in some special form of massage, whether Reflexology, Swedish, Shiatsu or other, or in the science and art of facial massage (which here would need at least a chapter to itself) of course you and your partner can add in, or can substitute, suitable techniques whose purpose and action are known to you. But make all movements *rhythmic, gentle in their beginning, heedful, and an expression of* YOUR LOVE.

Checkpoint 3

- This Erotic Massage is meant not only to heighten pleasure, but also to intensify for both partners a physical and emotional awareness of oneness.

- Four types of hand-action are listed for use in this massage. Reflect on the nature and stated use of each, so as to follow the massage directions with understanding and purpose:

  1. *Stroking* soothes fatigue and circulatory discomforts. (It can also be very sensuous.)
     Note the general direction of stroking the limbs: towards the heart in each case.

  2. *Kneading* stimulates a cleansing circulation of blood in stiff muscles or fatty areas. Rotary kneading of the abdomen is a good toner; *note the direction:* clockwise.

3. *Tapping* tones and stimulates. It can be gentle, as when any stretching of the skin must be avoided, or firm as when toning the spine.

4. *Handling* involves taking a small part of the body and pulling, rolling, squeezing or otherwise manipulating it for the purpose of stimulation.

- Beware of causing pain! Recognize pain as being nature's warning signal: *stop at once anything which causes it.* If something you do causes pain and you know of no normal reason why it should, have a physician's opinion about it.

- Avoid unnecessary talking during massage; both partners should learn to appreciate the non-verbal rapport which can be built up in silence.

- Invest in a massage table if you and your partner make massage part of your way of life. *No other way can the benefits of massage be given or received to the full.*

- To perform any massage, always use a lubricant.

    For regular use, have a vegetable oil: castor oil, olive oil, cooking oils without chemical additives and with unobjectionable smell, can be used straight or mixed.

For occasional use, dry skin benefits from the use of hydrous lanolin. *(Not pure Lanolin!)*

* Any lubricant used can be perfumed with an aromatic oil. Make sure neither you nor your partner is allergic to any you choose.

* Avoid giving shocks, in erotic massage most paricularly:

   Don't put cold oil on your partner's skin.

   Begin any strong actions gently; never prod or punch.

   When moving around or beginning a new series of movements, make sure your partner knows just where you are all the time.

* Note the value of the Charging Breath. Practice the way to perform it:

   Your mouth closed, *take a deep, steady breath. Hold this breath* for a moment.

   Open your mouth directly over the focal point for the charge.

   Intending to convey warmth, vitality and love, *breathe out gently and completely.*

* This Erotic Massage can be used:

   (i)   *Not completed*, developing from any point into a sex session.

  (ii) *Completed*, then followed by the Central Column Energizer and by dynamic sex.

(iii) *Completed* but not followed by sex, because *love grows on desire*.

(iv) *Completed*, then followed by an energizer if desired, before ritual action or a play situation.

●   Before the Erotic Massage, the partners should take a shower.

●   The massage procedure consists of four parts:

Sections 1 through 2, partners standing for preliminaries of breathing and energization.

Sections 3 through 7, recipient lying face upwards: stresses and psychic congestion are reduced in the feet, and thus in the whole system.

Sections 8 through 14A, recipient lying face downwards: soothing and sensuous movements on limbs and trunk are followed by stimulating and toning action at both physical and psychic levels for the spinal column. Head and ears are massaged to relieve stress and to promote sexuality.

Sections 15 through 23A, recipient lying face

upwards: massage of the relaxed and toned recipient enters its most specifically erotic phase. Attention is given to key neural centers and pressure points, culminating in some manipulation (which is still true erotic massage) of the genitals themselves.

- Throughout the massage, make all movements rhythmic, gentle in their beginning, heedful, and an expression of your love.

Study Points
4

1. Fantasy — in fashions & decorations, in architecture & furnishing, in entertainment & everyday "game-playing" — is a necessary refreshment to the human spirit, a restoration of balance in lives that have to be orderly and disciplined, an opportunity to relax the inhibitions that Civilization places upon primitive instincts and feelings.
   a. Fantasy is likewise valuable in Love/Sex/Romance. It is a way to give expression to the "primitive" in each of us, for " . . .whatever is primitive in a person has a rightful place in the love-life."
   b. The "primitive" is really the *basically human:* the simple and natural connections to the World of Nature and the Life-Force flowing in all things.
   c. To touch the primitive in each of us is to open channels to inner levels of the psyche.

2. Fantasy can be adapted from the primitive as seen in the "outer world" — from cultures different than your own (for "otherness" always touches the primitive levels within), or it can be "invented" to include whatever your imagination conjures up that is appealing to the primitive in you.
    a. Primitive-fantasy can be limited to your love-making, or it can be extended to include much more. It can be a re-discovery of things that are natural, and of the Beauty within Nature, and within the natural person.
    b. Two factors should have a vital place in your primitive sexual fantasy-playing: nudity and flamelight.

3. Fantasy should call forth an expansion of the ways in which you express yourselves: body language, tonal qualities of the voice, gesture; dance, song, drama; costume, masks, cosmetics, body paints, etc.
    a. If at all possible, extend this further to include a special room, or even a cabin or tent, as a place for your primitive fantasy-playing.
    b. It also can be extended to include a natural approach to diet and exercises — an awareness of the primitively healthy and attractive physical body. Nudity helps free energy and enables the skin to breathe, and motivates us to seek health and body-tone. "Thinking primitive" gives us directions to natural and wholesome foods.

4. The "guiding directive" behind primitive fantasy-
playing is to make yourself feel more primitive,
and to make yourself more attractive to the primitive
in your partner.
   a. A "courtship dance" makes an ideal setting for
   this. It involves movements and rhythm, music
   and drama, costume and ornament, and whatever
   else you may be inspired to provide or do — all
   intended to "win" your partner.
   b. Making contact with the primitive in yourself
   and in your partner is to bring inner levels of
   the psyche into awareness. *"Because you can find
   your inner nature reflected in your partner,
   sexual love gives you a key to it."*
   c. It is your true nature to be happy! Through your
   shared Love/Sex/Romance relationship you can
   discover forms of expression in which your emotional and physical natures participate free of false
   restraint and inhibition.

5. The opening of channels between the different levels
of your being requires free-flowing energy. In
addition to the Psychic Energizers, the techniques
of Erotic Massage and the Charging Breath, *playing
primitive provides other ways to build up energy
and send it flowing through and between you.*

6. A wonderful way to bring the primitive into your
life, and to contact natural energy sources, is to

restore connections to the natural world.

a. Salutations to the Sun, at dawn and at sunset.
b. Celebrations of the Changes of Season — with seasonal foods in a feast, with traditional folk dances and rituals.
c. Birthday celebrations for you and your partner.
d. Nudity when possible.
e. Taking showers, especially together.
f. Dancing.
g. Singing.
h. Exercising together.
i. Crafts. Making simple objects, rejecting the overly complex and learning to make and do things simply, with natural resources.

All these approaches to a natural way of life will free energies within you, help you discover your own self, and bring about a renewal of your natural connection to the World of Nature.

4

Fantasy 1:
The Primitive

Much as most of us appreciate the comfort and convenience of civilized life, there's something in a lot of people which wants to rebel against these things. There's a feeling that we are losing some essential quality of life: the part-hostility and part-kinship of the natural world in which, and by which, human beings have come to be what they are. To some extent we cope with this feeling by having some experience of the natural world during vacations, and for the rest of the time we fall back on fantasy.

Marie-Antoinette, who had been brought up in her Viennese girlhood to accept luxury and elegance as natural conditions in her life, used while she was Queen of France to play at being a "shepherdess" in the gardens of the Tuileries; her husband the king preferred to spend his spare time as a locksmith in a rather secret workshop he'd had fitted up for the purpose. But Marie-Antoinette was by no means the first adult make-believe shepherdess. Centuries before, in the high cultures of Grecian Sicily and of Imperial Rome, leisured and luxury-loving men and women had a fancy for being herdsmen and dairymaids, and the great poets Theocritus and Virgil wrote exquisite "bucolic" verses to please them. (Though the "luxury" of which they had wearied would seem simple enough to most of us — no refrigerators, no electricity, no automobiles — !) All the world has heard, too, how the great Caliph Haroun al-Raschid loved to leave his palace and walk in disguise among the artisans and beggars of Baghdad.

In our own civilized environments we experience something of the same kind of role-playing. It appears in the different types of "ethnic" fashions in dress which affect us every few years, in the use of chunky, rough-hewn styles in architecture and furnishing, in returns to the "primitive" in all the arts. These things seem from time to time to be necessary refreshments for the human spirit.

Above all, this necessity exists in matters of sex. Elegance and sophistication have their allurements, and there is no limit to the mind's ingenuity in that respect; but in fact we can only go just so far along that road before we feel we are becoming "too artificial to live," and one way or another a balance has to be regained.

Hence, such stories as those of King Cophetua and the Beggar-maid, and Lady Chatterly's Lover, have an endless fascination for the civilized imagination where true primitives would either shrug and say "So what?" or else would simply blot out the lovers as taboo-breakers without a second thought.

We are not too much concerned, then, in our love-play, with serious researches into what genuinely primitive people really think and feel, interesting and important though those studies are in themselves. We are inescapably what we are, and the leaven of civilization, even by our awareness of its existence, has unavoidably made some differences in our outlook. Yet a great deal of the primitive remains submerged in each of us, and we have a real need from time to time to give it expression. This is vital in love and sex, because whatever is primitive in a person has a rightful place in the love-life. You and your partner should meet these two basic aspects of each other!

You can play at being any primitive pair of characters you choose, but, equally, you may well prefer to be your own unique kind of "primitives" in whatever type of setting you want to imagine or make.

You can center the game entirely on your love-making, or you can make it mean more to you — and be much more fun — by bringing in other activities such as eating and drinking, creating an abode and so on.

However you play it, two factors should be prominent in your "primitive" experience: nudity, and (if you can manage not to set fire to yourselves or to your dwelling) flamelight.

It's as well to know what your ceilings, upholstery and so on are made of, as some popular types of solid foam are not only very flammable but give off deadly fumes if they do catch fire. Reasonable precautions are therefore desirable. However, if you think there's any danger, you can most likely still have your flamelight, either in the form of a fire in a regular open fireplace, or as candles in glasses located where arms and legs won't overturn them.

A good plan for your flamelight frolics is to clear the floor of anything you or your partner might trip over, and then to reduce any other forms of lighting to a minimum: that way, you'll be able to see just what the flames are doing. You don't want worry about this to spoil your fun, so the best idea is to have the whole scene visible at a glance.

Nudity and flamelight are a deeply sexy combination; nudity alone lacks the same appeal. As medical students and art students often find, a total and unhindered view of the unclothed human body can cease to be a turn-on in a surprisingly short time. A modern woman has written:

> *"To the pure, all is pure"* —
> *Sure!*
> *But if you seek a lover,*
> *Cover.*

Just as see-through garments excite, or garments with heavy swaying fringes (affording a continually changeable view of the wearer), so the naked body can excite

very powerfully too, *when it's present in all its nearness and touchableness and yet is clothed in the changeful, unpredictable now-you-see-it-now-you-don't of flamelight in the dark.*

However, facial expression can also become enigmatic as flamelight plays its tricks. A warm smile can become suddenly remote, eyes can become strangely luminous or can be mysteriously hidden. It's as well to remember this, and not to depend too much on facial expression to convey your feelings in flamelight sessions.

In fact, the evidence is that facial expression meant little to cave-people, for instance. They often didn't bother to give features to human figures, and it was very much later — when representational art had developed to a high degree — before even the "archaic smile" was shown. Today we are learning again how much more we can understand of a person from the tone of the voice, and from posture and movement, than from a facial expression or words which may only come from convention or habit.

So while you and your partner are playing primitive, you should take full advantage of this great chance to expand your means of expressing yourself, to "loosen up" in body language and in voice. You'll not be making intellectual speeches to each other, so you can practice using few and simple words, expressing yourself as fully as you can in tone and action.

Gestures, developing into dance, drama and the use of masks, were undoubtedly among humanity's earliest means of expression. These arts are somewhere in all of us, deeply buried or nearer to the surface: find them! You and your partner will be more complete as human beings, as well as more complete as lovers.

Besides voice and gesture, there's also communication by touch. Nudity and flame-light give special scope and use for this means of expression, too, which is sometimes instinctively understood more rapidly than speech. A touch on one part or another of the body can say "Stand up," "Come to me," or "Go over there;" it can say "Trust me," or "Be strong," "Speak!" or "Listen!" It can say "I love you." Try by a touch to convey what you want to say to your partner, and be sensitive to what your partner says in this manner to you.

Take pleasure, too, in your partner's body; not just by looking at it, and not just by directly sexual contacts. Other contacts are pleasurable, too, both to give and to receive. Touch the back, the arms, embrace the shoulders, gently explore with your fingers the intricate sensitive molding of throat, knee or ankle. Discover how what you can feel supplements what you can see, in the way the muscle-structure of the waist rises out of the bone-structure of the hips.

Let your partner enjoy making similar explorations of your body too; remember, each body belongs to the two of you! This is more leisured and less methodical than even the most sensuous massage; although Erotic

Massage has its place too, perhaps as a preliminary which can be enjoyed, on one occasion by you and on another by your partner, to usher in some of your sessions of playing primitive.

You both can further enhance the potentials of nudity, and can create some fascinating effects either on yourselves or on one another, by the use of body paints. This is very much in keeping with playing primitive. You can make complex designs if you wish, perhaps enhancing the contours of the body, perhaps to give curious effects in dancing or in performing various movements. Or you can use various colors in simple and striking ways. Or, again, you can have fun changing each other's designs. What matters is for you and your partner to experiment, to fantasize, to discover yourselves and each other in ways your everyday life hasn't allowed you to do.

If you both like this game, and want to make it your special love-game, you can build a lot into it.

You might even decide to set aside a room in your home, or a cabin or a large tent, to be your "primitive" dwelling. Have no conventional pieces of furniture in it, but do have sitting and lying-down arrangements which both of you find comfortable.

You can paint, make in clay, carve or otherwise achieve suitable adornments for this dwelling. You can make or obtain simple garments for yourselves, since you may not want to stay quite naked whenever you play this game. (You may want to have a primitive day, for instance, or a primitive week-end or even a longer period, and the change of attraction between sessions of nudity and seeing each other in picturesque scanty garments can add a new dimension to your play.) This is a particularly good chance for the man to have the fun and the good experience of making his own attire; he is not, after all, expected to go to business in his creations, and will most likely come up with something spectacular.

All these things can either be done according to your own imaginations and sense of "rightness" (which is after all the way real primitives set about it) or you can model them in the style of one culture or another which simply interests you, or with which you have ancestral or incarnational links. There are plenty of books on different ways of life, as well as costume books as such, to help you.

Whatever you do, however, don't lose sight of the main object of the game, which is the promotion of your love-sex relationship. "Is it authentic?" is a less important question than either "Can I be my uninhibited self in this?" or "Will I look attractive in it?" *Don't overdo the quantity of the garments, either: see them continually as* enhancements *of your body rather than as coverings.*

Having planned your own costumes, why not plan your own dance — a primitive courtship dance, for instance? (You can court each other any number of times, the more the better!)

The whole object of a courtship dance, naturally, besides introducing some inviting sexual movements, is to give the man a chance to show off his best points to the woman and to let the woman display herself most favorably to the man. This supposes each will be looking at each, and that condition is hard to fulfill if *he* is also tapping a drum and *she* is playing a home-made recorder. So, lacking a band of primitive musicians to play for you, you'll do well to accompany your dance with appropriate "canned" music, whether you prefer something from *"L'Apres-midi d'un Faune"*, or a Hopi dance, or your own cassette of your own sounds on (best fun of all) home-made primitive instruments.

Really make something of these occasions! Unlike real primitives, you don't have to do your dance in front of a crowd of watchful mammas and papas who want everything done just as it was in days gone by, nor in front of a crowd of critical kid brothers and sisters. So you can go all out to win your special partner — that man or that woman over there — and use everything which will make you primitively more attractive for the purpose. Flowers, perfume, incense sticks, body-paint, cosmetics, barbaric jewelry, as well as your movements and gestures and such attire as you may have chosen, should all be directed to that purpose.

Human bodies aren't always just as we should wish

them to be, and sometimes no amount of wishing seems to make them so. A primitive courtship occasion, however, gives you a superb opportunity to revise your partner's mental picture of you!

NEVER MIND WHAT HE OR SHE KNOWS ABOUT YOUR APPEARANCE, THIS IS A CHANCE TO START OVER.

Clothing can be more than an ornament; it can be a disguise, a change of outline, a director of attention *to* or *away from* itself. To know what can be done with even scanty attire is much more to the point than sighing after physical perfection.

So if you want to make the most of your hair, but your hair doesn't have the makings, devise a fantastic head-dress for yourself. If you have funny feet, wear sandals. *But also consider what your best points are, and with paint or jewelry highlight them.*

Mata Hari was one of the most notoriously seductive and irresistible women born in this modern age. She had beauty and intelligence, and was a skilled dancer with intense erotic appeal. She planned her own dances around mythological and fanciful themes, designing them to show off almost every aspect of her body, and her costumes were made to her exact requirements by a leading Paris fashion house. But although these costumes were made for private performances rather than public ones, and were for the most part enhancements of virtual nudity, *she never bared her breasts.* The rest of her attire might be of the sheerest fabric, but always a trim little bra or bodice covered her bosom.

The only reason for this concealment which can be guessed at, is simply that she judged her breasts to be not up to the same standard as the rest of her superb body. Plastic surgery, which would probably be the answer for a woman with her resources now, was at that time not advanced enough to help. *But it has never been supposed or suggested that Mata Hari lost anything, either in appearance or in power of allurement, by this bit of mystery.*

So, for one woman "primitive" costume, when desired, might mean a leopard-spot two-piece bikini and a copper bangle; for another it might mean just a chunky necklace or two and a grass (or grass-*looking*) skirt. One man might choose only a belt of big metal discs and a pair of leggings; another might prefer a loin-cloth and sandals. *Study your style!*

At the same time, it's quite possible that some of the things you don't like about your appearance, if you know you are either over- or underweight for example, can be helped by exercise and diet. Maybe you've realized this for some time, but playing primitive will give you just the extra incentive you need to start on making those improvements.

If your partner has the same problem (which often happens) then instead of turning a blind eye to each other it's time you both began to turn a *perceiving* eye, and to help and encourage each other instead of sharing mutual excuses.

Playing primitive can be a good reason for eating sensible meals; whether your weight is too much or too little, empty calories are of no use to you and neither are high seasonings and artificial flavors. You may not want to go very "primitive" in your food, but at least you can take the occasion to eat plenty of uncooked foods (unprocessed cereals, milk, fruits, nuts, salads with a little lemon juice or cider vinegar for dressing) and you can experiment with things you might not otherwise eat, such as dandelion leaves in the salad. *But don't make a penance of natural eating!* Take one step at a time.

For people who have no specific problem to worry about but who simply don't look as young as they did — and such people do often seem to feel their bodies ought to be hidden from sight — a change in thinking may be all that's needed. This century is gradually developing a healthier outlook upon this and related subjects, but it can still be pushed a bit faster.

You may not want to go surfing, or to bake wrinkles into your skin in the sunshine, but you can and should let the air to your skin as much as possible. You can also find out what and how much exercise is good for you and do that regularly, to tone your muscles and keep your posture as it should be.

Many so-called "old age" symptoms are due to faulty posture, and most of the rest are due to faulty nutrition and/or faulty elimination, the latter again being often related to faulty posture. If you can correct these things you may not look like twenty but your self-respect will soar, and everyone else's opinion of you will be boosted too. (*That's Magick!*).

You sometimes hear intolerant young people — for that matter, you sometimes even hear intolerant older people! — expressing views that beyond this age or that age men and women *ought not* to dress in certain ways, *ought not* to be seen on beaches and so forth. NONSENSE! — a public beach is not a chorus line, and a well-kept body has a right to go where it pleases; and the more this is understood, the more incentive older people will have to take a pride in their looks, to keep fit and have fun.

Playing primitive has a lot in it, then, for everyone, young and old. It helps you let go of inhibitions and neuroses *which may not be* your *inhibitions and neuroses at all,* but may have been put on to you by people around you, who in turn were burdened with these things by people around *them.*

It's always only too easy for people to be persuaded they ought to be inhibited, limited, unhappy; whereas in reality it's their true nature to be happy, as it is the true nature of every living being.

To find one's true nature within oneself is to be

happy. Mystics can find this inner linking within themselves regardless of their outer circumstances, but they are always a minority. For you and your partner, however, the way is open for finding your inner selves reflected in each other, and so through your shared love-sex relationship to *bring through* your hidden inner happiness, into forms of expression in which your emotional and physical natures will participate.

Any opening-up of experience between different levels of your being, no matter how you achieve it, will require plenty of free-flowing energy. So will the interpersonal link-up of instinctual, emotional and higher levels between your partner and yourself.

YOU ALREADY HAVE SOME GOOD ENERGY BOOSTERS IN THE FOUR PSYCHIC ENERGIZERS, AND, IF YOU TAKE IT IN TURN TO GIVE AND RECEIVE THE EROTIC MASSAGE, YOU EACH GIVE THE OTHER SOME SPECIAL SEXUAL BOOSTERS BY THE CHARGING BREATH.

In addition, playing primitive can show you, or can bring out more clearly for you, some other ways to build up energy and to set it coursing through you and between the two of you; as well as ways of directing the energy when you have it. Some of these ways, if not already a part of your everyday life, will certainly be a great help to you if you decide to adopt them permanently.

THE BETTER YOUR HEALTH AND VITALITY, THE
BETTER YOUR LOVE-SEX LIFE.

THE BETTER YOU CAN CONTROL AND DIRECT
YOUR ENERGY, THE MORE MAGICAL WILL BE YOUR
WHOLE EXISTENCE.

1.   *Nudity* helps energy. Your skin gets a chance to
breathe and to live as it should, and this contributes
to health and vitality. Your skin is an important *organ
of respiration.* (A main reason why a burn over a large
area of the body is so dangerous, even dangerous to
life, is that the damage prevents a considerable part
of the skin from *breathing.* The old story of a person
dying after being gold-painted for a carnival is founded
on fact, and is explained by the same phenomenon.)
Regularly changing from night garments to day garments
and vice versa, and varying this only by immersing the
body in water, can, over a long period of time, discourage
the skin from functioning as fully as it should.

2.   *Taking showers* helps energy. You can give showering a place in playing primitive, because with this form
of bathing you're less tempted to use artificial bath-
essences and over-hot water. Too, when you shower,
*you enjoy a physical toner and energizer from the
negative ions with which you deluge your skin.* Water
coming from the faucet and collecting in a bath doesn't
have them; water forced through a spray *does,* just as
the spray of a natural waterfall does.

(Showering with your partner, and the sensuous

feel of being soaped and afterwards towelled by each other, is a sexy delight you shouldn't miss!)

3.   *Dancing* helps energy. Dancing opposite each other sets up a powerful loosening and surge of energy between you. *Do one of the Psychic Energizers before a dance and see what happens!*

4.   *Singing* helps; it calls forth energy as well as co-ordinating the singers inwardly by means of rhythm and united purpose. All sorts of communities, primitive and other, have created "work songs" to gain those very benefits. You and your partner may not feel like creating songs — although you might feel well able to put your own tune to existing words, or your own words to an existing tune — but anything from a love-song to a rousing chorus, which you can get into the habit of singing together, will help get your mutual energies flowing and increasing.

5.   *Exercising together* helps energy. To some extent, it helps in the same ways as dancing, but the whole "feel" of it is different. Exercises you can really do *together,* making similar or complementary movements, are very good for developing co-ordination between you in the psyche as well as in the body. Some isometric exercises are designed on man-and-woman lines, and are great for discovering unexpected kinds of reciprocity between you. (So, if you're up to it, is playing at Tarzan and Jane on a pair of trapezes; but don't take a crash course by mistake!)

6.   *Celebrations* are an excellent way of directing

energy as well as building it up.

Primitive people (and you, when you're playing primitive) usually have something to celebrate. It's of little importance in primitive life whether today is the seventh or the seventeenth, or whether the time is 10:30 or 11:45. It matters very much, however, whether the sun is rising or setting, and whether it's Spring or Fall. It's important that the humans involved should be in harmony with the natural forces of the occasion, and that those forces should if possible be brought into harmony with the humans.

Hence a number of celebrations, in which, incidentally, the humans are frequently brought very closely into harmony with each other. That has always been recognized as one of the most attractive and exciting things about celebrating any occasion; its other fascination is the adventurous feeling of stepping, together, for a short time into a greater dimension than that of simple material existence. Material objects become symbolic of spiritual realities, words and actions take on a deeper resonance than might have been at first perceived.

You can expect, if you follow out this line of activity, to make your own discoveries of this kind; here we shall only make a few suggestions for your imagination to work on.

(a)   *Morning and Night*
Many western people, as well as great numbers in

the east, sincerely salute the Sun at dawn and at sunset, or on rising and before going to bed. Ancient Egypt set a sublime precedent, recognizing the sun as the chief symbol of spiritual power in our world, just as the physical rays of the sun are the source of light, warmth, health and energy.

As one of our Christmas carols proclaims, taking its inspiration from Hebrew prophecy (Malachi, chapter 4, verse 2):

> *Hail the Sun of Righteousness!*
> *Light and life to all He brings,*
> *Risen with healing in His wings . . .*

The sun essentially represents the Eternal made manifest in the material universe and in the transient moment. "Hail to thee in thy rising, O Creator of thine own manifestation!" declares an Egyptian salutation which has come down to us in hieroglyphic text;* and although in a sense dawn and sunset are "always the same," yet every dawn and every sunset, every day and night, is different and unique. "Thou Beauty most ancient yet ever new!" wrote St. Augustine of the Eternal; in words which every student of the Qabalah could relate to the Solar manifestation of Deity, and which every lover can relate to the delicious contrast between the familiar and the excitingly unknown in the loved one.

So a minute or two of real salutation, in whatever

---

* A simplified rendering, true to the spirit of the Egyptian Salutations for sunrise and sunset is given on pages 173 and 174 of *The Magical Philosophy* Vol. I, (Llewellyn, 1974).

words and to what Name you choose, can very well mark morning and night for you and your partner, and help you recapture some of the most primal of human impulses. (If, on vacation maybe, you can do this in open country, under the sky, it will be an unforgettable part of the private world which vacation trips enable you to build up together.)

(b) *Changes of Season*

, To take note of the year's seasons, with their differing weather, activities, and pace in the processes of living, has always been for humans both a necessity and a fascination. Making this a part of our personal lives, ushering in each season with suitable decorations, costume perhaps, and a seasonable meal, is an excellent way to keep in tune with Nature.

The idea of seasonal foods is a bit meaningless in the supermarket, but if you grow your own fruit and vegetables you can still find deep personal significance in having a little "feast" of "the first peas" or "the first peaches." (Solemnly tasting these can be very meaningful for the children, too.)

But your attunement to the seasons may have a wider aspect. What are the typical activities during each season, or marking a special seasonal day, where you live? Talk it over with your partner and see if you can do the same or similar things in some particularly original way. Playing primitive can enliven your everyday outlook as well as your intimate time together!

(c) *Your Birthdays*

Celebrating one's birthday is a custom which probably goes back to before the western world kept written records. Likewise, helping someone near and dear celebrate his or her birthday is an essential part of the custom; it is also a very evident and delightful way of saying, "I'm glad you were born!" This is a natural time for reflection, for true appreciation of this person whose coming into incarnation is being celebrated. *The greatest birthday gift is love.*

Your birthday, and your partner's birthday, are full of sexual interest for the two of you. If it's your partner's birthday, you are greeting a person who has just entered into a new year of maturity and experience. There will certainly be some new aspect, physical or emotional or both, in your relationship with that person. If it's *your* birthday, then it's you who are in some sense a different person from the self of your previous birthday, and, again, your relationship with your partner is in some way brought into a new phase.

Either way, you both have a special incentive to test and try, to find out what the new ingredient in your relationship will prove to be.

In many ways, the primitive or just basically human influence we have been tracing out can spread in your life far beyond the limits of your sessions of love-sex pleasure.

Find the happiness of simplifying one aspect or another of your lives: ask yourselves (and each other) what are the real values underlying this or that sophistication. You don't have to reject everything complex or civilized, but your playing primitive should heighten your perception of where the complexities and sophistications are to be found. You should question these things so as to arrive at a real personal understanding of why you want them and what's good in them.

Whenever you can, too, do the simple things people have always done.

Look (you and your partner) at dawn and sunset, sun, moon and stars: not as you scientifically know them to be, but *as you do in fact see them*, as people have always seen them. Gaze with wonder, with awareness, with reverence, with a renewed sense of beauty.

Find again the talents you have, which modern technology may have prevented your developing. If you want to make moccasins for yourself and your family, or to work a handloom, or to make pottery, or ceramic or wooden figurines, or papier-mache masks, *do these things!* You'll surprise yourself and others by creating objects of beauty, and you'll smooth out that secret resentment most of us have, against the way civilization has robbed us of the chance to exercise so many of our human abilities. Besides, you and your partner will both have a clearer view of the person you really are.

That way lies better life, and better love.

Checkpoint
4

- Playing primitive is a way to explore and enhance your love-sex relationship. It's also a way to give expression to the feeling for a primitive way of life which is probably submerged in you and your partner.

- You can play at being members of some particular primitive culture, or you can follow your own ideas of how to be primitive. You can play this game just when you make love, or you can extend it to include meals and other activities. *You and your partner can make decisions on these points — or simply start playing and see how the game develops.*

- Two vital erotic ingredients in playing primitive

are *nudity* and *flamelight,* and they can be combined excellently.

- While playing by flamelight, practice making yourself understood by simple body-language of gesture and touch, and by expressive tones of voice. Practice, also, understanding your partner's communications in the same conditions.

- Use body paints to heighten your appreciation of the experience of nudity.

- If playing primitive becomes a regular part of your life, set aside a room, cabin or other area for it, and have the fun of providing it with suitable decorations.

- For non-nude sessions, make your own primitive garments. Study your best points, and see how attractive you can make your outfit.

- Do a primitive courtship dance. If you can make a tape of yourselves playing primitive music on home-made instruments, that's an ideal accompaniment! Then show each other how alluring you can be while dancing to its rhythm.

- Playing primitive gives you a great chance to revise your exercise and diet programs!

- Recognize the right of every person, old or young alike, to take a pride in the body, to keep fit and have fun.

- To be happy is the true nature of every living being. No matter what your outer circumstances, your inner self is happy *right now*. The mystics stay happy through contact with their inner nature.

- *Because you can find your inner nature reflected in your partner, sexual love gives you a key to it.* Through your shared love-sex relationship you can both bring through your inner joy into forms of expression in which your emotional and physical nature will participate.

- For bringing through inner levels to awareness, you need energy.
  For energy, you need good health and vitality. The better your health and vitality, the better your love-sex life.
  The better you can control and direct your energy, the more magical will be your whole existence.

- Build up shared energy with your partner by frequent psychic energizers and erotic massage.

- You can release energy by nudity — by showering

— by exercise. You can control and direct energy
as well as releasing it, by dancing — by singing — by
celebrating special occasions with suitable actions.

●   Find the proper place in your life for the primitive
(or "basically human"). Look into what's complex
or civilized, decide why you want it and what's
good in it. Appreciate the natural world. Develop
your talents. Discover yourself, discover — and be
discovered by — your partner.

Study Points
5

1. Romance is a state of intensified feeling in which two persons' all-pervading interest in each other opens them to new discoveries and perceptions of the wonder and beauty in and around them.

   a. At the same time, romance frees us of some of the restraints upon our perceptions that our ordinary every-day life demands, and depends on.

   b. Romance is never free of sexual awareness. Even when a person is alone, if beauty and wonder have evoked a romantic mood then there is such an "awakening" of the whole person that sexual awareness must be part of it.

   c. It is sexual awareness, while not always involving the physical level, that sharpens our perceptions, that invokes hidden potentials, that enriches our whole being, making us more alive!

2. It's a principle of magick that *"by employing as a cause something we have seen as an effect, we can produce as an effect that which we have seen as a cause."*

    a. Just as a romantic involvement created a situation in which you found beauty and wonder in each other and in the world around you, so — by placing yourselves in situations where your surroundings are exciting, wondrous and beautiful — can you create a new mood of romance.

    b. By placing yourselves in situations that really appeal to you, you will find that new aspects of yourselves are invoked and expressed — that undeveloped potentials within are given new opportunities for expression — and you may well find yourselves "falling in love" all over again.

3. This discovery of, and delighting in, new aspects of each other is a way to release still more of the hidden potentials within you, a process that has already been started with the primitive fantasy-playing of the previous chapter.

    a. It has been said that "love brings out the best in a person" — but it's also true that love, and romance, bring out *more* of a person!

    b. Love, then, is an important part of the growth and development of every person — well worth "working at," and cultivating romance is one of the easiest and most enjoyable ways to enhance your love, and sex, relationship.

4. The creation of a romance fantasy must always contain something of the erotic and the mysterious.

    a. Mystery gives the imagination something to work on. Mystery depends upon simplicity — rather than detail — in the props you use, and upon a change of pace: the changing of the various signatures that are part of our familiar identity — perfume, hair-style, costume; our usual choices of music, food, the things we talk about, etc.

    b. The Erotic is sometimes another name for the romantic. In choosing a costume, for example, that is part of your new fantasy remember that you want it to be seductive, that it must enhance your attractiveness. You want the fantasy to end up with love-making, so make sure that the "means" you choose lead to the "end" you want.

5. "Games" are valuable ways to encourage romance. And certain games have become so firmly established in the history of romance that they possess a power to initiate the entire fantasy for the two of you — while yet encouraging the many personal variations that are important to this form of magick. One of these is the game of "the Mysterious Strangers."

    a. Create a situation in which each of you pretends to be a stranger to the other — but *that* stranger is someone interesting to you, someone you wish to captivate!

b. Augment this scenario in as many ways as the situation allows: perhaps you can wear masks, certainly adopt mannerisms and behavior your partner doesn't usually identify with you — even be "outrageous," knowing it's all in fun; make up stories as to who you are, wear a costume fitting your pretended role, etc.

c. Role-playing is an effective way to bring into consciousness aspects of the psyche that lie deep in the unconscious. As has been shown previously, adopting roles that contrast with your normal self can loosen many of the fetters to your expanding awareness.

d. The game of "Mysterious Strangers" adds depth and meaning to your role-playing, whether it be a situation created by a masquerade-party, the opportunity created in a vacation, the drama involved in a seasonal festival, or the setting chosen just "for the two of you," as a candle-lit supper in your own private place.

5

Fantasy 2: The Romantic

What is romance?

We can speak of *a* romance, meaning a novel full of imaginative and idealized situations, or meaning a rapturous love-affair, a "real-life romance"; but romance as such, romance in the abstract, is less easy to pin down. Romance is a quality which doesn't so much depend on what you do as on how you do it and with what accompaniments.

Matthew Arnold's old definition of romance as "a sense of background" has been harshly criticized, but really there's a lot of truth in it. Much romantic feeling is created by an awareness — maybe a sudden awareness — that your actions, your words, your thoughts and emotions and your very being are part of a larger unity, part of a "picture".

A sense of romance can, for some people, break

through into their perceptions even when they are alone, even when they are not in love with anyone; but such people usually have a great and deep love for life itself, and a great zest for living. More generally we associate romance with lovers; and in their heightened perceptions and their more emotional way of looking at the world around them, we can find a clue to what romance really is.

Civilized human beings have a habit of isolating themselves, wrapping themselves up in their hidden thoughts and feelings. In the artificial world in which many people live, this is frequently necessary for survival. You don't have to be too impressionable while shopping. You need to keep your ideas of what you *want* isolated from what other people *want you to want*. The same applies when you eat out, the same in business life. So people learn to isolate themselves, to close down, to keep the rest of the world out.

Except — frequently — on vacation; and except when they fall in love.

A vacation is often an artifically-planned "silly season", a time when people not only relax, and open their hearts and their minds, but also spend their money recklessly and break a lot of their self-made rules for living. It can be beneficial, or it can put people in touch with nothing except the artificial environment they've chosen for the purpose.

Falling in love is a different matter because basically there's nothing artificial about it. A man and a woman in love — especially just falling in love — become sensitive not only to each other but to whatever catches their attention in the world around them. The particular season of the year, whichever one it may be, becomes beautiful to them; whatever song is popular at that time tends to become "our song." It's a familiar joke, but true none the less. They are living a new world — each other's world — and, as for a blind person who has just gained the power to see, every detail imprints itself on their consciousness.

Now: by understanding this, as with many other situations in life we discover a way to make real magick — love-magick in this case — by reversing the procedure. *By employing as a cause something we have seen as an effect, we can produce as an effect that which we have seen as a cause.*

By putting yourselves in a situation where your surroundings strike freshly upon your consciousness with a sense of beauty, of wonder and excitement, making you and your partner aware each of the other as part of a world of mystery and delight, you can give your love a fresh impetus, a new vigor and intensity.

You may ask, *"Yes, but is this worth doing? If we are only acting our respective parts in a fantasy show, a piece of make-believe drama, won't the glamor fade when we return to being our workaday selves?"*

NO, THIS NEED NOT HAPPEN. "GLAMOR" FADES, BUT THE EFFECTS OF TRUE MAGICK REMAIN. YOU

NEED NOT BE JUST PLAY-ACTING!

If you and your partner choose situations which really appeal to you both, these will awaken and call forth real aspects of yourselves which might not otherwise find expression.

A diamond fresh from the mine is "itself," but nobody can appreciate the fire in it. If it is skillfully cut with a number of facets, it sparkles. The more facets it receives, the more ways it takes the light, the greater its brilliance.

A mono recording of music can be "true" to the tone of the original, but it lacks life and luster. A stereo recording brings out its depth and variety. Two speakers will present it well; three or four speakers show it to be even richer and more delightful.

Neither the gem nor the music is falsified by being presented to better advantage. Even less can you and your partner lose by discovering, exploring and delighting in more and more aspects of each other.

You may not have thought before of how many "selves" you have, how many "selves" your partner has. We have mentioned in Chapter 1 that each person has, in the deeps of the psyche, both a male "self" and a female "self", with one or other of which the conscious personality identifies itself. (Although of course it's possible, and helpful, to be to some extent conscious of the nature of your "unadopted" Animus or Anima.) At less profound levels the inner scene is, however, much more complicated than that.

Supposing a few circumstances in your early life had worked out differently: you might very well have taken up a different type of career from your existing one. That would have made differences in your life, in your experiences and so very likely in your whole outlook. Supposing you'd grown up in a different land, or in a different kind or degree of civilization? Supposing your education had been different?

None of these things would have altered the essential YOU-ness of YOU, which, looking back, you can recognize at least as having been there through all the varying moods and viewpoints of your infancy, childhood and adolescence; but they would have made big differences in the way you seem to the outer world, even in the way you seem to yourself.

Yet all these different potentials are there in you somewhere, for the most part unexpressed and maybe even unrecognized by you. And the same, naturally, applies to your partner's potentials; so how many possible variatons in personality do the two of you have between you?

Let's find means to bring out the hidden fire in the diamond, the stereophonic depth in the music!

Playing primitive — which you may still be continuing, or may mean sometime to return to — will have released some of your hidden possibilities; but you certainly have many more.

You can take for your "scenario" any historical or geographical setting, past or present, which has high romantic appeal for you and your partner, if you are both imaginatively enough into science fiction, you can make a background for your romance right outside this planet and/or in the remote future, should that please you! There's only one condition: *whatever you choose has to have a really emotional appeal for you, not merely an intellectual interest.*

You might feel it would be an interesting challenge to prepare something like a regal banquet of ancient Egypt, or to re-create the feeling of Dracula's castle in Transylvania; but those things will contain no romance for you unless you get sufficiently involved emotionally, to be able to come to life in the setting you formulate.

On the other hand it's certain that any changes in your emotional experience, any new doorways of perception and awareness that you open up, will shift the focus, not just for you as a person but *for you as a sexual person*, and will give you and your partner a chance to react to each other in new ways.

Supposing the fantasy personality you find easiest to slip into, doesn't correspond to your partner's favorite role? Often that does no harm. Think of a costume party! A "theme" is sometimes dictated by host or hostess — or to some extent by the occasion — but the parties which are most successful, where people really "get off the ground", are usually the ones where individual preference is not too severely bound: where a toreador may dance with a lady pirate and a Hawaiian princess may flirt with a Cossack. No matter how much one person's fantasy differs from another's, each still gives license and validity to the other by its very existence and presence.

Where the occasion sets a general theme, that's fine too if it is one which has built itself into everyone's imagination, so as to be "second nature". This often happens at Hallowe'en. Most of us have some kind of shadow-self which enjoys the chance to proclaim itself in a disguise, as a Witch or a Skeleton, a Black Cat or a White Phantom or a Demon, and we can enjoy meeting each other on the same terms — *for that occasion.*

So with your fantasy-selves of the kind we are discussing in this chapter. Here, it's desirable to keep sight of the fact that what you want to build up is not simply fantasy, but *romance;* whatever means you choose should always have something both erotic and mysterious about them, to steer this venture to its right end.

An air of mystery is tremendously helpful. Its main value is to give the imagination of your partner something to work on, and this is far more potent than if you yourself carefully supply all the details of your assumed character. Imagine a nineteenth-century type of stage-set, with doors and windows, tables and chairs, statues and plants "realistically" painted in: and then the whole illusion could be destroyed if a spotlight caught it from the wrong angle, or if somebody happened to kick a canvas "wall". Then think of a more modern type of set, where a few suitable "properties" and some carefully-illuminated space do duty for the whole scene, and you can percieve that the latter is the more potent. Its "reality" is not there on the stage where a careless movement can shatter it, but unassailably — when once it has been built up — *in the spectator's imagination.*

So your air of mystery can not only save you the chore of having to invent too many details for your fantasy; it can also save you from spoiling the romance by bringing in everyday matters which are, here, quite irrelevant. It's of no use for you and your partner dressing yourselves in Greek tunics and bright scarves, and sitting down on a pile of cushions to a repast of retsina and black olives, to the sound of exotic Eastern Mediterranean music, if you are going to discuss Junior's school report or whom you are going to invite for Thanksgiving.

If you enjoy your little feast, listen to the music, pay each other some appreciative compliments, quietly establish emotional and physical contact and make love, it can be a memorable occasion. Carry the atmosphere of your fantasy into your love-making. *You are two other people:* perhaps try out positions and rhythms of movement you don't usually use.

The woman — and perhaps the man too — can make a subtle but quite effective "difference" to such an occasion by using something other than her, or his, usual fragrance. Many people nowadays are in any case getting away from the idea of one perfume or cologne per person for evermore. They recognize that a fragrance is, at best, not the "signature" of a person so much as the signature of an aspect, a facet, a mood of that person.

In the present instance, that "signature" is something to beware of, for even if the conscious mind doesn't notice it the unconscious mind will, and for success in our romantic fantasy the unconscious mind is the one we have to capture. A woman may like her man to smell of Brut or of Chanel Pour Homme, for example, but it's rather a strain on her powers of fantasy if her Greek lover and her eighteenth-century French lover and her favorite crew-member of Starship *Enterprise* all smell alike!

Certain romantic fantasy-games are of so much importance as to rate special mention. One testimonial to them is that they've captured the imaginations and woven themselves into the emotional life of numbers of people, for centuries; and they still have immense power today.

One is the Mysterious Strangers game.

As a matter of fact, no matter what costume you may be using, or whether you are in modern clothes or starkers, it's always fun and a good booster for love-making if you and your partner can pretend now and then that you've only just met for the first time. You want to attract each other, so you begin by introducing yourselves, exchanging biographical details, making conversation so as to be able to ask about each other's tastes and interests, and the rest.

This gives both of you a chance to show what interesting, attractive and sexy people you are, and to look each other over with a fresh eye. (Many couples will want to arrange a few hours' notice before standing up to this mutual scrutiny.) But, presented in the context of a Carnival encounter, it has a special charm.

The Mysterious Strangers

It's worth while to play this game wearing real Carnival-style eye-masks. As a variation, the woman could either wear a yashmak or one of those Mexican veils which are, in effect, a diagonal yashmak and are so potently seductive as to have been officially banned, long ago, from public wear. But the eye-mask has much to recommend it because it hides habitual or give-away expressions of the eyes, and thus helps the sub-rational nature of each player to a feeling that his or her partner really has somehow taken on a new personality and become transformed to a truly mysterious stranger!

The association of the eye-mask — and an older type which covered the nose as well, looking somewhat peculiar but so doing more to disguise the features — with the Mardi Gras Carnival goes back for centuries. In Venice, as elsewhere, the Carnival, coming just before the fasting and penance of Lent, in and after the Middle Ages became a riot of festivities and an unequalled occasion for romance, secret meetings and

sexual freedom. Besides the people who welcomed the chance to wear masks to aid them in intrigues they'd planned beforehand, there were always plenty of people who set out with no specific program or partner in mind; people for whom the music, the stage-shows and dancing, the costumes and the masks themselves spelt Romance, breathing an atmosphere which made any chance adventure possible.

The young, the not-so-young and the distinctly-not-young-at-all, the rich, the less rich and anyone who could find themselves suitably festive clothing, would all participate somewhere in the crowded assemblies which packed themselves into the ballrooms and the taverns and the narrow streets, and on to the bridges, the gondolas and the marble stairways which bordered the canals of the wakeful city.

Not only an intimate dinner-table, or the solitude of a doorway or a buttress-angle, but the crowds themselves gave occasion for kissing and hand-clasping and embraces of every kind, some fleeting, some prolonged. Whether for a brief while or for life, men and women were pledging themselves as devotees of Love. It was Carnival time.

There were always, of course, some stay-at-homes: people who through age or ill-health or some coldness of heart or of principle, took no part whatever in the celebrations. Among these (according to a traditional story) had been for some years Gregorio di Rovigo and his wife Teodora. The were neither old nor sick, but a formal lifestyle and a great preoccupation with civic ambitions had pushed love out of their lives; they'd forgotten their interest in each other, without becoming interested in anyone else.

One year, however, perhaps Carnival time (which depends on the date of Easter) was later than usual; or perhaps the warm winds of Spring arrived earlier. For whatever reason, as the festivities approached Gregorio felt disposed to venture forth and sample them. He was tired of the solitude of his study and other rooms; his wife had her own suite and he saw little of her these days. So he astonished his tailor by ordering a splendid brocade cape to be privately delivered to him at short notice, and when the time came he quietly slipped out, disguised in the cape and a mask, to take a look at the entertainments.

At a certain stage in his wanderings he received a shock. Suddenly he realized he was looking at a dress which had been made for his wife some months previously. Now it was adorning a vivacious young woman who was being very freely embraced by an unknown youth; and on looking attentively Gregorio recognized the girl as Teodora's personal maid Giovanna. Clearly, Giovanna had borrowed the dress and had slipped out to enjoy herself. Gregorio was not concerned to interrupt the couple's pleasures — primly he decided it would be too undignified to admit he'd noticed them and what they were about — but what did concern him was the question of how in the world Giovanna could have taken the dress, put it on and left the house without Teodora's knowledge? For assuredly his wife would not have consented to that escapade.

Where, then, had Teodora gone? An unwelcome answer to that question suggested itself to him.

These thoughts made Gregorio's powers of observation rather sharper than they might otherwise have been. Instead of taking part in the dancing as he'd intended, he found himself moving — almost hurrying —from one gathering to another, swiftly and analytically looking over all the women there present.

Then, suddenly, he saw her. A dance was just ending, and Teodora was being escorted to a seat by an elegantly-dressed man at least ten years Gregorio's senior: she gave the stranger a ravishing smile. It was certainly Teodora; her face was masked, but her back was what he'd recognized at first glance. She was wearing a dress he'd never seen her in, but the poise of her head, the line of her shoulders was unmistakeable. Even the wide hooped skirt couldn't disguise the swing of her hips.

He felt distinctly hurt. A young gallant, that he could have understood. He'd have been jealous, but now he felt insulted as well. Why should a man more than ten years his senior be so confident, so attentive and so plainly attractive to Teodora? Why, he, Gregorio, if he bestirred himself, could — could —

His decision was made. Disguised as he was, he'd teach his foolish wife a lesson! *Just because she'd been receiving courteous bland attentions from a man who was* (Gregorio told himself) *probably unable to give anything more, did she, still handsome as she was, think she could safely venture at large in the festive, lustful city?* He'd show her! She'd find out what *could* happen!

He slipped up behind her and laid a hand on her bare shoulders, almost imperceptibly catching the little vertebral bump at the base of her neck between his first and second fingers. Instantly, before she looked at him, she knew him. He'd caressed her neck like that so often in their younger days! Perhaps he'd forgotten now, perhaps he'd never been conscious of doing it, but that movement of the fingers told her plainly: Gregorio. She turned to him, but he gave a formal bow, as to a stranger.

So her foolish husband was out flirting in the Carnival (she thought) *and had accosted his own wife without recognizing her?* She knew well enough he was too prudent to mean anything really scandalous, but how far did he think he could play with fire? All at once the idea of seducing him attracted her tremendously: she'd teach him a lesson! She smiled coquettishly.

The night gradually mounted to delirious sweetness. Secure, as they each thought, in disguise, they could do outrageous things to each other and were surprised to be met with equal warmth. They danced, they kissed, they feasted, they embraced ardently while a gondola carried them over the lantern-lit waterways. Then firmly, despite her half-hearted protests, he blindfolded her with a scarf.

Taking her by a roundabout way to their home, he led her silently up the back stairs and into his bedroom, and removed the scarf. Simultaneously they unmasked.

"I knew it was you, all the time."

"All the time, too, I knew it was you. I believe what you say, because I'm telling the truth myself."

"I believe what *you* say, without hesitation, for the same reason."

But the dawn broke upon such passionate love-making as they'd never before known. Their masked adventure had lifted them into a new life.

You can enact any number of themes in your "Carnival of Venice," or you may just want to see what comes of it. Each of you, confronted with a figure which is made truly enigmatic by a mask (and which has an added strangeness caused by seeing *you* masked) will find new significances in the question *"Who are you?"*

Or you can play it another way, with or without masks, at a party or any festive gathering. You may be able to contrive not even to arrive together — but in any case, when you are there, circulate quite separately among the other guests. Take a positive interest in people and in what they say to you: *you are taking time out from your partnership.* You hostess will love both of you for this; on a social occasion, couples who cling to-gether certainly don't *zing* together! So long as you're both happy and smiling, no-one is likely to think you've quarreled; and besides, sooner or later the two of you will meet up.

When you do, try to give yourself the "he/she doesn't know me" line of Gregorio and Teodora, and act as if you, too, thought your partner a particularly fascinating stranger. *Be captivating!* Remember, you are rather more mature and experienced now than you have been, and it's likely that neither your partner nor even you yourself know *how* fascinating your present self can be. Surprise both of you!

Don't treat your partner in just the way you feel sure he or she will find acceptable. Sometimes a man or a woman knows, or sees in a movie, or reads of, some specially alluring maneuver which would be such fun to try, if only his or her mate had "less fixed ideas." Well, now's the time to try it; after all, you aren't supposed to know, yet, what *that new person's* ideas are. Be more daring: don't conform to what you *expect* your partner to expect. And of course, since things are on that footing, you'll not be surprised if you too recieve some unusual endearments. You may indeed *end* the evening "clinging together!"

Who are you? is a wonderful question. You and your partner can give it many wonderful answers.

Another game you may want to consider here is *the reversed-role game.* The man plays at being the woman, the woman plays at being the man. For some couples this game is fascinating, bringing a great deal of release from hidden tension, and a consequent sharp rise in sexual pleasure. *At the directly sexual part of*

*the proceedings, the couple can continue their assumed
roles but quite usually they return with a much intensified zest to their usual relationship.*

The amount of enjoyment and of emotional fulfillment which a couple finds in this play has little to do
with either their ordinary sexual attitudes or their
physical appearance. Sometimes people who are near
the mid-region of sexuality will easily take a turn, so
to speak, around the center-point, more for amusement
than anything else; a somewhat feminine man and a
somewhat masculine woman may put considerable art
into changing roles at a private costume party, for
instance. Quite often, however, men and women whose
ordinary experiences are virtually an extreme of maleness
and of femaleness respectively, will be the ones who
find the greatest delight in giving their opposite-sex
characteristics a holiday from their usual state of severe
repression.

This type of play has been recognized, together
with its beneficial tendencies, from quite ancient times.
Legend has it that Herakles — or, to give him his Roman
name, Hercules — in the course of his turbulent career
of mixed heroism and irrational violence was told by an
oracle, as a penalty or a healing or both, to sell himself
into slavery for three years. This he did, and was bought
by Omphale the widowed Queen of Lydia. Some versions
of the story tell how the massive and preternaturally
powerful Hercules, in obedience to Omphale, put on
woman's dress and in that guise played music to entertain

her and spun yarn to be of use to her. She meanwhile took over his lion-skin and club. Evidently she took a keen personal interest in the proceedings, for at the three years' end she married him and bore him a son.

Whatever ancient customs went into the making of that story, there's obviously a recognition in it of the complex hidden background underlying the more usual patterns of sex and love.

Romance, however we interpret it, always involves at some level a degree of role-playing. Most often it involves a heightening, not a reversal, of the couple's ordinary sexual roles, but even that heightening lifts it out of everyday existence. "Romantic" clothes for men, for instance, are usually very masculine; "romantic" clothes for women are usually very feminine. Perfumes, too — a most romantic adjunct — emphasize sexual attributes. Perfumes for men usually evoke some masculine association: "outdoor" smells of wood and aromatic plants, tobacco fragrance, undertones of leather, male-toned odors such as musk; while perfumes for women are usually predominantly floral-toned, and woody or citrus aromas are considered suitable for "sporty" or day wear rather than evening. Wearing "romantic" clothes and perfumes, the man or woman is expected to behave *and to feel* appropriately.

That brings us back to a salient point of this chapter; *as you behave, so you will in fact feel,* if the chosen role is anyway "right" for some facet of you.

Thus you and your partner will be enabled to experience, to appreciate and to love, aspects of each other's being which might not ordinarily have been apparent.

It's vital, when weaving this kind of spell for yourselves, not to break it by interposing unsuitable actions. Erotic massage and psychic energizers for example — *things which should certainly be kept up* — must not spoil the atmosphere of a romantic session. *If they come in naturally and spontaneously,* well and good. Omphale, or Cleopatra, in a wanton mood may bid Herclules, or Antony, to be her masseur. Or an Arabian Nights prince may ask a magical massage from a mysterious maiden who has been sent to serve him. *Most usually, however, you'll find it easier to maintain "atmosphere" by performing your massage and/or energizers as a prelude to your play sessions.*

The quality of romance takes some thought and care to achieve, but it well repays that trouble. It is, certainly, a role-playing; but it strikes deep responses of reality, and so brings out meaning, as well as adding embellishment, in life.

Checkpoint
5

- Being in love causes people to see more glamor and "specialness' around them, and in each other. So you and your partner, by making yourselves and your surroundings more glamorous and special, can magically step up your love relationship!

- You have many hidden "selves" which can surface in different settings, and so has your partner. Enrich your relationship by meeting a few more of each other!

- In your romantic meetings, *include* both erotic and mysterious effects. *Exclude* everyday and unrelated matters.

- *On such occasions, you and your partner are two*

other people. Plan some details — names, clothes, hairstyles, toiletries — whatever you can to help build up this feeling.

- Pretend you and your partner are meeting for the first time! It's a good tonic for romance on any occasion.

- Carnival masks help immensely, hiding habitual expressions of the eyes and making you and your partner really "unfamiliar" to each other.

- Enact your "mysterious strangers" episode over an elegant candle-light supper in your own home — or go separately to a party and meet "for the first time" amid the festivities.

- The reversed-role game can give great enjoyment and emotional fulfillment, above all to couples whose everyday life gives no scope for anything but the stereotyped images of man and woman.

- Keep up massage and psychic energizers, but don't let them spoil a romantic game by coming in at the wrong place. If they fit into the mood of the game, that's fine; otherwise, use them as a prelude to your romantic activity.

Study Points
6

1. The capacity for prolonged love-making and multiple orgasms — for both men and women — is neither myth nor dependent upon rare physiological attributes!

   a. This capacity can be learned — and the learning process is not difficult, nor is its achievement exhausting.

   b. This capacity in no way detracts from your mutual pleasure — rather, it adds to it enormously.

   c. This capacity, and the practice of prolonged love-making, brings many additional benefits: increased physical — and emotional — health, extended youth, more physical — and psychic — energy, more joy in living and loving.

   d. This capacity adds to the total integration between the partners — reaching to all levels of the psyche, achieving greater depth of union.

2. To understand the program developed in this chapter,
   you have to realize that a man can have orgasm *without* ejaculation.
   a. The program to achieve the self-control needed
      for delaying — or avoiding — ejaculation while
      enjoying one or several orgasms, involves cooper-
      ation between the partners.
   b. For the woman, this may require some psycho-
      logical adjustment: allowing the man to set the
      pace, and encouraging him in his own re-adjust-
      ment from the more "macho" kind of sex which
      many men believe is expected of them.
   c. Ejaculation control includes changed expectations,
      self-control and self-awareness, breath-control,
      use of certain muscles, and — as needed — use
      of a certain pressure point.

3. Ejaculation control opens a far greater range of
   sexual activity and ways to experience and express
   love and achieve peaks of ecstasy beyond previous
   experience.
   a. Many positions for love-making may be tried —
      and each may involve new sensations, new psychic
    · contacts, new psychological releases.
   b. The rhythms of love-making, the moods, the in-
      tensity, etc. all may be varied — many within
      even a single, long "Night of Bliss."

6

Nights of Bliss

Nights and days of love, long sessions of love-sex joy with no doubts or fears, no sudden moods of seeming indifference which are really exhaustion; rapture soaring above rapture into a fulfillment beyond all words which gradually merges into the mutual tenderness and cherishing of complete harmony and peace.

Isn't that what all lovers want, what you and your partner want?

Games, masquerades and fantasies can do much to heighten the fun and delight of sex, and to help interpret you and your partner to one another in various roles and in different aspects of your being. But, by themselves, their power is limited.

Don't you wish you could play for longer, enjoy for longer?

YOU CAN. There is a skill of love which can

greatly extend your pleasure, and which, although of necessity it remained long unproclaimed, some people in the Western world have certainly known for many centuries. You can combine it with what fashion of love you will, with playing primitive or with the numberless guises of romance, or, as will appear in the next chapter, with the games and fantasies of another traditional mode of love.

Usually upon hearing of prolonged love-sessions, of orgasms multiplied through the night, or of day-time raptures when two lovers fall into each other's embrace on a lonely hillside or in their living-room, people react by stating, "That's delightful, but I couldn't stand the pace!" — "I'd think four times in a night would be my limit," say the women. "A week of that would kill me," say the men.

THEY DON'T HAVE TO BE RIGHT!

If you and your partner are in normal health you can, by learning these ways and the underlying principles, enjoy long, blissful hours of love and sex together. To people who, because of some problem of health or age, have to indulge sparingly in sex as generally understood, the application of these principles can be a life-saving, love-saving boon.

For the unusually robust — those men and women whose capacity for sex enjoyment is distinctly more developed than average — it can be added that these principles are an excellent safeguard, enabling them to continue the enjoyment which means so much to them without fear of depleting either their powers or their enthusiasm, onward into an old age whose signs are likely to be slow in appearing. (It's well known that nothing truly "keeps a person young" so effectively as a sound interest in living, good motivation for staying healthy, and a good ongoing love relationship.)

The main practice may need some patience in learning, as there are some points for the man to attend to especially, some for the woman; but the rewards are great for both.

Initially, there is a point of vocabulary to settle. In most contexts, when people speak of "male orgasm," this term is understood to include the emission, or ejaculation, of semen. Sometimes the word "climax" is used as the equivalent of "orgasm", and the same understanding applies.

Webster's *New World Dictionary* makes the truth of the matter clear: as a special meaning of "orgasm" it gives "the climax of sexual excitement, as in intercourse, usually accompanied in the male by ejaculation." However, the linking of orgasm and ejaculation can be less close even than that. As Joshua Bagby finely states it in "Forum" (November 1981):

A man who is confident, secure, trusting and loving in his sex life transcends unloving . . . sex. . . . Many men experience multiple orgasms before ejaculating (some men are so satisfied from this play they don't even bother to ejaculate!)

The truth which is embodied by these words of an authority on human relationships is an important one. It's well known that a man can, when circumstances are good, become accustomed to experiencing numerous orgasms without ejaculation. *That means:*

(1) Increased self-respect and self-confidence on his part. A double pride, both in a full sex life and in awareness of self-control.

(2) No harm resulting to his work or sport in consequence of his active sex life.

(3) Instead, a real incentive in all his activities, a new joy in living.

(4) More sensitive and more prolonged physical enjoyment for both partners.

(5) More love and more real happiness, because mutual satisfaction will not blunt the edge of mutual attraction.

Many of the above points are likely to appeal to the woman also; so, additionally, may these:

(1) She is likely to discover her own capacity for sexual enjoyment to be far greater than she ever supposed; while at the same time, since male ejaculation is usually the most limiting factor in a couple's sexual program, she will incur far less than average risk of being left unsatisfied.

(2) Because the urgency will be taken out of sexual fulfillment, while the enjoyment of it is increased, there will be greater scope also to develop love's more

emotional and romantic aspects. Thus her feminine self-esteem and personal morale should very quickly soar.

Those are the most commonly experienced benefits of this form of intercourse. There are, however, a few difficulties to be looked at.

For the man, the chief difficulty is simply in achieving the desired ability. It is not too difficult, all the same, with some perseverance and the real will to achieve it; once the knack of control has been found, the difficulty is over. We shall come back shortly to that aspect of the matter.

An important factor is that the woman can help or hinder considerably. The couple need to have built up a good harmonious relationship, without any hidden resentments against each other: people use sex as a means of aggression or of revenge, either against their partner personally or against society as represented by their partner, more often than they realize.

Not only the man needs to make a sincere effort to achieve this self-confident, loving, cherishing form of intercourse; the woman also needs to have confidence in herself as a sexual person, and to wish well to her partner at all levels and in full sincerity. *She must not try to use sex so as to gain some advantage over him.*

To explain this further. One of the things the man has to do so as to learn this skill of love, is sometimes during the intercourse to slacken the speed and intensity of his thrusts. If the woman, desirous of reaching her own orgasm, is unwilling or unable to slacken her own movements, she will obviously make difficulties for him. By words or signals to each other the two partners should be able before long to get the situation mutually under control, and without separating their bodies to take a brief breathing-space before gently beginning the action once more.

The woman's problem in this may however be psychological rather than physical.

She may only recently have experienced the pleasure of sometimes taking the lead in sexual activity, and she may not inwardly feel willing to give up that prerogative. So when her man ceases for the moment to lead the action, she may automatically take the initiative, and intensify the movement instead of letting it subside.

Her best help here is in understanding and foresight. If she allows her man to set the pace just now, when he has physically a more difficult task than she has, she will gain immensely in pleasure and in privilege later as the lover of a happy, unworried, non-aggressive man.

IN THIS AS IN MANY OTHER MATTERS, WOMAN CAN ONLY BE LIBERATED IN THE MEASURE THAT SHE CONSENTS TO MAN'S LIBERATION FROM HER.

Again, the woman may unconsciously, or even consciously, be *unwilling* to let the man be able to avoid ejaculation. Despite the current emphasis upon clitoral pleasure, there is at least for some women a subtle physical reaction to the release of semen high in the vagina. But that sensation is not likely to give her sufficient motive for compelling the man to ejaculate at every orgasm, as against the advantages and the varied ecstatic pleasures to be gained by allowing him *not* to do so.

Her hidden psychological motivation in hindering his progress is likely to be that she fears losing a means of asserting her power over him.

This isn't a consideration to every woman of course, but it undoubtedly is for some.

It's an inescapable fact that the strongest man, in the moment of ejaculation, is helpless as a baby. At one level or another, a woman knows this. By withholding ejaculation, a man not only physically conserves his powers; psychologically, he also keeps control over his own destiny.

By forcing him to ejaculate, a woman can assume a position of both physical and psychological power over her man. This can be tempting: a reversal of man's sometimes unfeeling use of sexual power over the destiny of woman.

None of that, however, is what your love-sex relationship is about! It isn't MEANT as a means for the man to dominate the woman in her weakness, nor for the woman to dominate the man in *his*. Each partner should be respected by the other as a person with free choice; *that way, even though they may be wedded sixty years, every day and every night of those sixty years is a free gift of love, from each partner to the other.*

A final feminine problem we have to look at, is that a woman may actually *fear* increasing her man's capacity for sex. She may in the past have regarded it as one of his more selfish activities, and feel that one or two orgasms on any given occasion (which may be the most she has ever experienced) are as much as she wants. Nor need this mean that she is frigid.

Such a woman's point of view can usually only be helped by better experience. This book is about sex as a happy and shared thing, and the skill of love which is the present theme is a most essentially shared, tender and considerate way of expressing the love-sex relationship. It is true, admittedly, that many women, especially those whose experience has been strictly within the limits of one partnership, have never known more than two or three orgasms on an occasion; and have very likely been kept awake on some occasions, when they were tired out, because their man happened to be "in the mood".

When this skill of love is employed, no woman need be wearily kept awake in such circumstances, for her man will have no reason to fear he may not be just as ready to share pleasure with her the next night, or the night after that if she prefers.

Besides, she'll enjoy sex much more when she has

been aroused to her full capacity for it — and when she doesn't unconsciously hold back from arousal for fear of being left sex-hungry for a week after!

A pattern often encountered with a first experience of numerous orgasms is that a couple will go through the first four together. Orgasms 5 and 6 are instituted by the man, not against the woman's will but simply to her surprise; but then follow orgasms 7 and 8, instituted by the now thoroughly aroused and delighted woman; the last being the ultimate peak.

(There's no reason why the woman should not take the initiative when she feels like doing so in these sessions, provided she has let the man go through the *learning* phase at his own pace.)

About eight orgasms, if they are not taken one immediately following the other but are interspersed with periods of tender caressing and/or sleep, will carry most couples through an average night. Where there occurs a series of truly "multiple" orgasms, each following only a short while after the last, the "high" of ecstasy is likely to be reached sooner by both partners but it may not last so long or so effecively. Each couple can however only correlate their own experiences.

How, then, does the man begin practicing so as to achieve this skill of love?

The essential first step is for him to learn to delay ejaculation. Orgasm without ejaculation can be then anticipated as a natural development from that.

It is generally understood that delayed ejaculation is harder for a young man to achieve than an older one, but the basis for this seems to be simply that a considerable number of young men who have learned nothing of sexual control tend to ejaculate more quickly than is either convenient or pleasurable to themselves and to their partners. It doesn't mean these men are too young to learn, only that they particularly need to do so.

As against their inexperience in having sex in a controlled way, it can be said for thém that they've had less experience than older men generally have, of having sex in an uncontrolled way. The young men therefore have less to unlearn. They also have, or should have, their youthful resolution and enthusiasm to help them: they will be learning something which can lead them into a lifetime of happiness. (All this usually applies to their partners also, and their aid is of the greatest value.)

Whatever the ages of the couple, these are the steps to be taken:

A. The session should begin with a Psychic Energizer. *As a very general guide,* for this special purpose the Palm-to-Palm or the Feet-to-Feet Energizers are suggested for younger people, the Spiral Energizer or the Central Column Energizer for older ones, but no firm rules can be made.

B. As indicated above, during the learning stage it's *essential* that the man alone should have the directing of the session. He has to make prompt decisions based on his physical feelings, and, at first, the time taken in communicating these feelings and decisions to even the most sensitive partner can be too long. At the same time it is most desirable that the woman should know and be in sympathy with what the man is doing: that way, she too can practice control, and will neither try to take the initiative at this critical stage, nor mistakenly feel slighted.

C. Insertion should be effected without urgency and with all the help the woman can give; this done, there should be a moment's pause.

D. Thrusting should commence gently, and at first not deeply. When deep thrusting is done (not more often than once in some five or six thrusts) *it should not be allowed to increase the pace.*

E. Breathing should also be kept to a steady rhythm, not being allowed to increase in rapidity. The mouth should if possible remain closed. Should the man need to breathe more *deeply,* he can take his breath slowly right down to his diaphragm and breathe slowly out again; keeping up a definite rhythm of moderate pace.

F. Continuing the movement, he should pay attention to his physical feelings. If he feels likely to be caught up into an irresistible increase of pace leading to ejaculation, he should PAUSE well before reaching the point of escalation.

G. The simplest way to check the impulse is for the man to draw back to some extent — without withdrawing completely — and to tense the genitals, breathing evenly while doing so. Thus he should remain unmoving for a few moments until he feels the excitement pass. He may lose a little of the firmness of his erection, but this should return as soon as he recommences the thrusting. (N. B. This is the pause during which, while the man remains still, the woman must take care to do so also.)

H. Another way to check ejaculation is by the use of the appropriate pressure point. The point used here has been indicated in our erotic massage technique as stimulating arousal in man or woman; here, however, arousal already exists, and the same pressure point functions differently.

Without withdrawing at all, the man pauses at whatever stage of the thrust he will, *takes a long, deep breath*, and, while holding this, with two fingers of his left hand he presses *firmly* into his perineum. After a few seconds the urgency should subside.

No matter which way he does it, with practice the relaxing of excitement will enable intercourse to be carried on without ejaculation for longer and longer periods. *As soon as the man's unconscious mind gets the message that ejaculation isn't necessary for orgasm,* either or both of the partners will be able to experience and enjoy orgasm freely without provoking an ejaculation.

How long a time should pass, or how many orgasms should occur, before ejaculation is allowed to take its course, must depend on several factors: the inclinations of the partners, the age and general health of the man, the time of year and the climate all have some bearing on the matter. Generally speaking, as long as the partners feel all is well, it is. Men who are relatively new to this skill of love may experience some feelings of tension in the testicles after one or more sessions of intercourse without ejaculation, but that need cause no apprehension. Only if the overall sense of wellbeing seems impaired need a man suspect he may be going too far too fast in his program of abstinence from ejaculation; and that matter is easily rectified.

We have quoted earlier in this chapter the words of an authority as to the naturalness for modern Western man of orgasm without ejaculation. This can interestingly be confirmed in some words of Jolan Chang, on the same subject as relating to the ancient Chinese art of Tao: *Ejaculation control . . . takes practice to become proficient. Once mastered thoroughly, the body will adapt to it and it will become the most natural thing in the world.* *

Once control of ejaculation is gained, orgasm without ejaculation is achieved at will: a liberating

---

* *The Tao of Love and Sex: The Ancient Chinese Way to Ecstasy,* by Jolan Chang (E.P. Dutton, New York 1977)

experience for both partners. Then the full range of sexual activity is open to them as a means to express their love, without the specters of impatience and exhaustion, and all the fears attendant on them.

For you and your partner, this can mean the dawn of a greater and deeper mutual understanding in your lives. It can also mean longer, more frequent and more blissful sessions of love-sex pleasure, in which you can explore all the rapturous possiblities of physical union.

You can at your leisure explore all the positions; and if some of them aren't a success for you, it's no great matter!

Why are there so many?

The subject of postures to be adopted by a couple for sex has fascinated both East and West for centuries. The East has illustrated a great array, from the scholarly love-treatises of China to the intricate sculpures, often representing divine beings, of Indian temples. Many Oriental positions for sex are chosen for metaphysical reasons; in the West, the choice is generally made either for maximum enjoyment or for the sake of change and curiosity; a notable Western collection forms a painted frieze in a house of pleasure preserved at Pompeii.

Basically, however, for actual intercourse as distinct from complex embraces, there are only a few positions you need trouble about; if you and your partner haven't yet discovered your favorites among them and their possible variants, why not experiment?

There is the face-to-face position. In its most obvious form, this has the woman lying on her back, the man above: the so-called "missionary" position. That name however shouldn't frighten you, as this is the starting-point for some delightful variations, the woman placing her hands in various ways, or swinging her feet up to the man's hips, waist or shoulders; he meanwhile supports his weight on his hands, forearms or knees. Other forms of face-to-face positions can have the man lying on his back, the woman above, or both partners standing with one or other of them leaning against a support.

There is the front-to-back position — popularly called the "doggie" position — in which the woman lies on her front, or kneels or crouches, and the man approaches from behind. This can be uncomfortably cramping for the woman, and many will find it better to take up the same position relative to each other but with man and woman both lying on their sides (right side or left as may prove more pleasurable.)

They can also, of course, lie on their sides face to face as another position for intercourse.

Then there are the seated positions. The man can sit with his hips well forward, so the woman can lower herself on to his penis and sit on his lap; she is likely to find this most convenient for action and for comfort if she bestrides his hips and he puts his arms around her waist. Or the man can lie on his back, the woman kneeling astride him facing either his head (the "Greco-Roman" position) or his feet.

A particularly comfortable and satisfactory version of this position is the "Armenian" form: the man lies on his back on a narrow couch or bench so that the woman bestriding him can put her feet down on the floor at the sides, thus being less cramped and having better leverage.

Other positions tend to be only variants on these. For instance, the woman can sit, or lie, with her butt on the edge of the bed and her feet on the floor, legs parted. For a very slim or inexperienced woman this can make the man's entry much easier, but the result is, of course, face-to-face.

There's no one "best" position for everyone. *The object of all these positions and variations is to give different angles of entry, different pressures in different directions.* To begin with, different couples vary in what they *like,* and then besides that they vary in what they'll *get.* The bodily proportions of man to woman, woman to man, are different from one couple to another and every detail affects their sexual experience. So you and your partner need to do your own testing and choosing.

Even if you only decide on three or four enjoyable postures, that's enough to allow for an occasional change in the "feel" of intercourse, and for a few new experiments in varying these positions when you feel like it.

You can also try different types, strengths and tempos of thrusting: deep or shallow, strong or mild, quick or slow, with all the combinations of these

qualities, together with variations in direction: whether vertical, slanting to different degrees, side-to-side or round-and-round.

The woman's response likewise can be controlled and varied by her so as to color the mood of the session. She can be passive or passionate, playful and light-hearted or romantic and dreamy; she can be supportive or enticing or dominating, she can woo or set herself to be wooed.

Of any couple, it might be said that the whole range of sexual experience lies open to them. Of the couple practicing ejaculation control, this can be said with real hope of their exploring, should they so wish, a goodly proportion of that range. Whether that is their ambition or not, it can be confidently predicted that they will enjoy a special and lasting mutual passion, total pleasure and enhanced understanding in their love-sex relationship. Rapture soaring above rapture into a fulfillment beyond all words will indeed be theirs.

Checkpoint
6

- Your capacity for sexual enjoyment may be much greater than you think.

- Control of ejaculation takes some effort to achieve, but the incentives are great for both partners.
    During the learning period the man alone should direct the sessions of love-making and set their tempo. The woman's co-operation and understanding are essential for this.

- The chief psychological hurdle for both is to escape from old ways of thinking: *ejaculation isn't necessary at every orgasm.*

- When ejaculation control has been acquired, both

181

impatience and *exhaustion* will be banished from your love-making! Follow the stages of procedure as set out in this chapter.

• This liberation wiil allow you much greater scope for experiment and exploration in sexual pleasure: try out new positions, new styles of action!

• Keep up your fantasy games, erotic massage and psychic energizers; during the learning period, choose which energizers suit you best.

• Lasting passion, total pleasure and enhanced understanding between the partners are among the rewards of this skill of love; so, for more of love's rapture, make it your own!

Study Points

7

1. The Troubadours of the Middle Ages represent a special Western Way of Love as part of the Magick of sex.

   a. The themes of the Troubadours' songs may be used as the basis for fantasy games to explore some special aspects of love and sexuality.

   b. For the Troubadours, love was a bond far more important than the bonds of marriage; for us, this theme is a reminder that even within marriage love is to be valued more highly than the domestic partnership — and hence that the Game of Love is well worth playing!

2. The Game of Love involves the partners playing their roles as lovers "motivated entirely by love."

   a. This means putting aside — for a time, within the fantasy-play — the concerns of duty, the worries about security, feelings of self-doubt, selfishness, possessiveness, etc. in order to fully play the *archetypal* roles of lovers.

   b. While the Games of Love are fantasies, the effects in the players' lives and characters are indeed "for real."

3. The Troubadour Games "always carry overtones of devotion, of idealism, of sacrifice, or some form of privation to be endured, and of a reward not to be won by half-measures." Almost always a limitation of sexual activity is a feature of these games, "to heighten love by increasing desire."

   a. Playing these fantasies increases sexual attraction at not only the physical level, but also at the psychic and spiritual levels.

   b. In playing these fantasies, the partners develop self-control, and gain enthusiasm for love, and for each other — perceiving new qualities and gaining new understanding.

   c. Through playing these fantasies, the partners experience deeper levels of awareness and understanding that reach universal realities transcending personal limitations.

4. These Games can be used — in conjunction with the practice of ejaculation-control — to lead the partners from instinctual compulsions into genuine mystical experiences.

5. The themes of the various Troubadour fantasies out-
    lined in this chapter lend themselves to a wide
    variety of particular developments by the couples
    playing them.

    a. A real situation — as when the partners are
       necessarily separated from each other — can be
       used as the basis for a fantasy game.

    b. A fantasy game, or even an extended drama, can
       be developed from such themes as Master or Mis-
       tress and Slave, God or Goddess and Worshipper,
       the Chastity Pact, Rescue of the Captive Princess,
       Secret Lovers, Forbidden Love, Ordeal and Reward,
       Chivalry, etc.

    c. Such variations as bondage, flagellation and
       fetishism can be incorporated into the basic
       fantasies — both for increased erotic build-up and
       as a way of mutual understanding and release.

6. Many of the fantasies can further incorporate some
    of the practices you have already learned in the
    previous chapters: the visualizations, the psychic
    energizers, erotic massage, etc.

    a. The Charging Breath can be used in adoration
       and worship of the partner as the incarnation
       of deity. A slave can be required to give erotic
       massages. Cooperative efforts in mastering ejac-
       ulation control can relate to punishment and
       reward. A fetish could become a Lady's favor to
       her Knight.

7

Fantasy 3:
The Game of Love

The foregoing chapter, with its potential for developing the more leisurely, tender yet potent aspects of sexual love, opens a new level of experience: one in which desire becomes indeed love's ally, bringing a thousand subtle shades of appreciation of each partner by the other. This experience, in turn, is closely related in spirit to a heritage of fantasy which comes to us from Europe's Middle Ages: a heritage too strongly woven into the Western way of living and feeling ever to have died or to have become outdated.

These love fantasies, and games, which lend themselves to endless variations, were most popular in Europe during the 12th, 13th and 14th centuries.

At that time, and for centuries later, it could happen in various parts of Europe that even a nobleman's home might be little except four fortified walls and a store of weapons, with dried or pickled foods for emergencies and some straw beds; but in the Crusades which were then in progress Moslem and Christian were by no means all the time killing each other, and fine silken fabrics, velvet and brocade, with pearls, gems and exotic perfumes, were finding their way more and more into Europe. More and more singers and scholars too were able to translate, or to adapt, sensuous Arab love-songs; and people in every walk of life were learning to play instruments, mostly of the type of the lute, mandolin and guitar.

For most Europeans the music, color and pageantry of life had long been centered in the Church; now they were finding their own sources of delight, and were exploring new themes for song in the love of man and woman.

This was the great age of the troubadours, those highly talented minstrels, whether roving or attached to some great house, whose surviving lyrics have set so many problems for editors and thesis-writers in the present age.

Most of these problems need not concern us at all. Undoubtedly the troubadours sing in praise of several different modes of love, and undoubtedly some of their lyrics reflect their own lives, thoughts and feelings; but it should be remembered (as it often is not) that these men were usually professional. They sang to please. If they pleased an influential lady, that was all to the good; and doubtless as with our present-day pop stars this did result in some genuine love affairs, fortunate and otherwise. In the main, however, if they were to continue their careers, their lyrics had to express sentiments people wanted to hear. They had to be welcome to some section of the society of their time, to their special "public" in fact.

Interestingly, the love and the situations their lyrics portray are usually very different from the simple and frank mating-scenes which were popular in earlier French lyrics. Here we have stories, or implied stories, of lovers vowing an endless devotion which not only survives, but thrives upon, a varied and unrelenting series of barriers to their union. One would think these medieval poets were making trial runs for Manzoni's "Betrothed." And these themes were promptly taken up, repeated, echoed and elaborated with eager delight through all the Western world.

Doubtless these songs about separated lovers and delayed unions fitted real-life circumstances for some couples. Men departing for the wars, and their wives or sweethearts, would for instance like to hear and sing songs about lovers whose hearts grew only fonder as distance separated them. But Europe's stay-at-homes delighted almost insatiably in similar themes, and a great many troubadour lyrics have come down to us which develop the idea in ways which soon became stylized and traditional.

Most of these songs, less realistic than the ones about men going to the wars, were quite obviously not

meant to be taken as anything but creations of fantasy,
and to be used as a basis for futher fantasy.

This is how you too can employ them.

The intense reality of fantasy to the minds of
medieval people is something many of us are beginning
to recapture today, even though intervening centuries
lost it. Cervantes set out to ridicule it in "Don Quixote,"
but people of the present century by-pass Cervantes
and take the Don to their hearts.

Present-day fantasy has shown us that we can live
in the world of Luke Skywalker, that we can renew, too,
the world of knights and dragons, and of maidens whose
valor is expressed in other than earthly strength. So
likewise, therefore, we can when we please renew the
fantasies of the troubadours and thus explore, as they
did, some special aspects of Love.

A pre-condition of troubadour fantasy is that the
partners are NOT supposed to be husband and wife.
This idea can cause some problems for couples who *are*
lawfully wedded, if they happen to be literal-minded
or scrupulous folk as well. But it makes sense.

To begin with, in the days of the troubadours most
marriages in Europe, as in some regions still, were
arranged matches. An arranged marriage can certainly
be as happy and as love-filled as any other, but often
it is not; and often it is precisely the sense of compulsion which spoils it for the partners.

But in any love-match too, if the partners aren't

watchful, that same sense of compulsion and of duty can creep in, when once the marriage vows have been taken, and can spoil their union too.

That doesn't say lovers ought not to marry, nor, certainly, that a married couple ought not to be lovers; but simply that *the partners ought not to regard their legal bond as the chief thing which holds the two of them together.* For happiness, they must think something like, "We are here together now because we care for each other" — NOT "because our duty as married people requires us to keep up this relationship."

IF A MARRIED COUPLE WANT TO BUILD UP ANY KIND OF MAGICAL RELATIONSHIP TOGETHER, THEY WOULD DO WELL TO AVOID MAKING EVEN MENTAL REFERENCE, IN THEIR MAGICAL ACTIVITY, TO THE FACT OF THEIR BEING MARRIED.

It is Love which soars on wings of inspiration, while Duty walks with heavy feet.

As it happened, there arose in India somewhat later than the time of the troubadours one of the many cults of Krishna; this one had — apparently by pure coincidence — in its poetry some of the outstanding characteristics of troubadour thought and sentiment. There, in that Oriental cult, we find the same insistence that the lovers must not be, or for cult purposes must not consider themselves as, husband and wife. The wife (the *svakiya* woman) is regarded as being motivated by duty and by heed for her reputation; the mistress (the *parakiya* woman) is regarded as being motivated entirely by love and willing to sacrifice all for her consuming passion. Edward C. Dimock makes the spirit in which this ruling should be taken abundantly clear when he points out that the cultists did not invent this classification of the two kinds of woman: *"svakiya* and *parakiya* are types of woman who can appear in drama."*

The concern here, then, is not with earthly reality nor with the many diversities of experience in earthly life. Here we have "types" in drama, in fantasy; "archetypes", indeed, recognized by the psyche as existing in the endless serial-drama of its secret inner world.

In truth we all, men and women alike, have both the *svakiya* and the *parakiya* within ourselves, although one or the other will be more apparent and more developed in this or that individual. What both the Eastern mystics and the Western troubadours are saying is that in the love-adventures of their fantasy worlds we must, men and women alike, separate ourselves from the selfish, doubting, insecure and possessive emotions which make captive both the experiencer and his or her partner — cease to identify with the *svakiya* in ourselves — and identify with the *parakiya* which is likewise in us, the confident, inwardly liberated being

---

* *The Place of the Hidden Moon: Erotic Mysticism in the Vaisnava-Sahajiya Cult of Bengal,* by Edward C. Dimock, Jr. (Univ. of Chicago Press, 1966).

for whom the sole purpose of loving is to love.

There is evidence that the fantasies embodied in the troubadour songs were tacitly known to be games, games to be played as fantasy with regard to the situations they presented, but "for real" with regard to their effects in the players' lives and characters. (Much as competitive sports are meant, not to be real combat, but to develop the players' resourcefulness and courage as if they were.) Because of their nature and purpose, these troubadour games always carry overtones of devotion, of idealism, of sacrifice, of some form of deprivation to be endured and of a reward not to be won by half-measures. They certainly increase sexual attraction — that was recognized — but attraction which is not at physical level alone, but also at psychic and spiritual levels. Thus the partners are aided in developing self-control while at the same time gaining enthusiasm both for love and for each other. This is a true development of the Magick of Sex!

You and your partner will find some of these fantasy games in particular can add color and sparkle to the situation when you are gaining practice in the method of ejaculation control given in the last chapter. There is, in fact, a distinct similarity between the heightened passion, tenderness and inner relatedness attained by the lovers in that skill of love, and the qualities which the troubadours proclaimed as the result of their "pure love." That love, by definition, excluded intercourse but was generally understood to permit, if the lady granted it, all other intimate contact. Their fantasy games were therefore designed to lead the minds of lovers away from the instinctual compulsions which were taken as inevitable in the earlier love-songs; and so the troubadour fantasies are excellently suited to couples in the rather similar situation of training themselves out of the habit of emission at every orgasm.

It is of course doubtful (and has frequently been doubted) whether *all* the adherents of the Cult of Love *always* adhered strictly to the limitations they set for themselves. Some did, evidently; the record of the inner experience and development of those who followed the way of "pure love" is too exact and too psychologically sound to be based entirely on fiction. But after the four or five centuries during which these fantasies were worked over by men and women of every temperament in every part of Europe, it is unlikely that *any* interpretation would be without precedent.

There is, therefore, likely to be something in these fantasies which you and your partner will wish to use as a basis for games and play-situations, whether you are following the delayed ejaculation practice, whether you are interested in abstinence from sex or in the mystical developments of sexual experience, whether you are into, or want to try, bondage and/or flagellation, or whether you simply seek new games and approaches to add variety and perspective to your love-life.

Because of the wide variety of ways in which these

fantasies can be applied — and evidently have been applied — by different couples in different circumstances, we must necessarily give them a certain breadth of treatment, with just sufficient indications to make clear the situations in which they can best be used, or some of the possible variations in interpreting the fantasy. If, however, you perceive and wish to follow any other interpretation, you are entirely free to do so.

The one requirement for using these fantasies in their traditional spirit, is that both of you should have joy in what you do.

Here are outlines of the best-known troubadour fantasies, somewhat modernized. Every poet or singer adapted them as he pleased; you should do the same.

(1)   You and your lover are parted
The evident occasion to use this fantasy in play is when you really are parted; you can begin it just before one of you goes on a journey. (*Notice how the game begins with simple "make-believe", then goes on to give both partners some real practice in the Cult of Love.)*
You can imagine for yourselves some tyrant who has decreed your separation, perhaps just on account of your love for each other. Together you plan your reunion. (If in earthly terms you have to go on a business trip for a few days, you could for instance

declare to your lover — who perfectly well knows the facts — "In a few days I'll secretly slip back to you; how could I resist?")

During your absence you may very well think often and spontaneously of your lover; but all the same, set yourself some special *signals* for remembering, and keep them faithfully if only for a few moments at a time. Such signals might be,

(a)   When you hear a burst of bird-song, or (according to the season) when you see a lonesome winter scene or a remote night sky.

(b)   Whenever you hear another person's telephone ringing. (Not *your* telephone; that would be too much of a distraction!)

(c)   Whenever you hear a nostalgic melody or a love song.

(d)   At meal-times, saying "I eat this food to keep me in life and health until I can return to my lover."

(e)   At bedtime, saying "Now I enfold myself in thoughts and dreams of my lover, until the day." Picture to yourself the embraces to which you will return, and the limbs which will give them.

(f)   Each morning, say "Another night past, another day nearer to my lover."

(g)   Whenever you spend a few moments thinking of your lover in any of the above ways, visualize also for a moment as clearly as you can, your lover thinking of you and missing you. See

your desire for each other as a shimmering airy bridge which links each of you to the other. Desire is your ally!

If you are the one who has to remain while your partner goes away, you can do the same things, changing the words where necessary. You can also picture yourself opening the door (secretly!) at your lover's return. Meantime, you also should perform the "bridge" visualization.

(2)   Another game for when you are parted.
The fantasy may very well have it that you and your partner have never yet been lovers. The woman is held captive by some cruel despot, the man plans a rescue. (If you can keep in touch with each other by letter or telephone, this fantasy can gain a lot more force; but be discreet! Anyone chancing upon your conversations or correspondence might imagine someone has really been kidnapped!)

As the time for the rescue draws near, the hero and heroine become more romantically involved in the project, and in each other. The prisoner, bidding her rescuer not to delay, fervently promises him any reward he may desire. Does he accept? — or does he plan for an even more high-powered sequel (as the troubadours sometimes did) by protesting that although he knows what he would ask, he cannot bring himself to accept reward?

If he takes the latter attitude, his partner's response must depend on how the situation is understood between them. If for any reason they've agreed to a no-sex reunion, she will support his decision; otherwise, she may coax him to change his mind at once, or else they can play it by degrees as in (5) below.

(3) Mistress (or Master) and Slave

This favorite troubadour theme is another game which can be played more than one way; it makes, according to your wishes or requirements, a "straight" game for no-sex occasions, or it can be a limited-sex or controlled-emission form of play, or again it can be a highly-spiced competition-of-wills teaser, in which either (i) the man simply does his utmost to coax the woman to change her mind, or (ii) the woman forbids the man to approach her but takes care to make herself irresistible to him so that a sexual culmination is inevitable.

The point of the game is that the woman has absolute authority as to how much sexual activity she'll allow her "slave" to enjoy. Sometimes she allows him none at all, in which case she may command him to address her as "Master", as the troubadours sometimes addressed their ladies. (She doesn't in that case act the part of a man; the medieval imagination could accommodate itself to a female "master", just as, later, Christina was officially "King" of Sweden and Elizabeth I of England called herself a "prince".)

This game, which should keep a certain light-hearted humor, is varied according to its use:

(a)   in no-sex or controlled-sex situations, where the man welcomes some support for his will-power under guise of a game; in which case the woman should be supportive to him, not tantalizing or punishing.

(b)   as a bondage/flagellation game, in which case penalties may be given for "infringements", the players perhaps taking turns as "Master."

(c)   Simply for fun, in the interest of break-ing that "regular partners" routine. "Mistress" can limit "Slave's" activities in all sorts of ways; a medieval favorite was that they should go to bed together unclothed, and he might kiss and embrace her, but no more. (Of course, if by his actions "Slave" persuades "Mistress" to relent, the game ends at that point to the satisfaction of both players!)

(4)   Deity and Worshipper
In troubadour tradition, the lady was sometimes addressed and regarded as a goddess. Oftener she was described, in terms less rashly at odds with the es-tablished religion, as a symbol and representative to her lover of the Supreme Good; or as Dante described Beatrice as "a unique creation of the Holy Trinity."

The recognition of one's partner as the chief manifestation of Godhead in one's life has, however, such a vital importance in the mysticism of sex that besides mentioning one of its aspects here as a troubadour fantasy, we shall enlarge on the theme as the subject of the next chapter. This high perception can be experienced in abstinence, but it belongs in its fullness in the ambience of physical sexuality.

(5) The Chastity Pact

This is another medieval favorite. The presupposed state of things is that the couple have, no matter why, pledged themselves to keep chastity.

If that were "for real", plainly their best course would be to leave each other alone, but that doesn't occur to them. They decide, in a tantalizing progress of eroticism, that a caress would be allowable, then that a kiss would be allowable, and so on. At some stage they may decide that a little mutual "punishment" would prudently slow the pace, but eventually with one thing and another they settle for a modest episode of embracing, without intercourse, between the sheets.

Again, play this as you will.* This can be a no-sex or limited-sex game; it can be a controlled-ejaculation game, or, like 3(c), it can be a game of seducing your partner.

---

* This medieval tradition of unclothed but chaste kissing and embracing is put forward by Andreas Capellani in his *De Amore* (around 1180). For another sincere medieval allusion to it, see Malory's account in *Morte d'Arthur*(1485) of the marriage of Sir Tristram to Iseult of the White Hand. For a skeptical Renaissance allusion to it, see Shakespear's *Othello* (1604), Act IV, scene 1.

Checkpoint
7

- The Middle Ages, like the present time, were a period when fantasy was appreciated. We can take up again some of the fantasy games of the troubadours, and learn something from them.

- In these games the partners are imagined "not to be married to each other." *Love soars on wings of inspiration, while Duty walks with heavy feet.* Being lovers is a habit of mind, which you and your partner should cultivate!

- Limitation of sexual activity is a feature in many of these games, to heighten love by increasing desire.

- When you and your lover are parted, the "Bridge"

visualization makes desire a way to unite you!

- These fantasy games have a special value:
     In practicing ejaculation control
     In facing either voluntary or unavoidable
          sexual abstinence
     In combination with bondage/flagellation
          sessions
     For those who simply seek new angles for
          variety in their love life.
  (The games of *Mistress (or Master) and Slave,* and
  The Chastity Pact, provide exciting possibilities
  in any of the above situations.)

- If you and your partner are away from each other,
  instead of seeking "distractions" plan an effective series of *reminders.*

- Keep up your psychic energizers, the erotic massage and the fantasy games. These things are not
  only enjoyable and in various ways beneficial:
  They are also good practice in releasing and directing energy.

Study Points
8

1. "In the shared experience of sexual love, man and woman make the way of inner evolution easier for each other."

   a. An Initiation Ceremony is an intense application of Symbol and Drama to induce certain evolutionary changes within a short time.

   b. All initiation rites are modeled upon the essentials of experiences taken from life.

   c. The experience of sexual love is the most powerful of life experiences, and the most faithful in its reflection and transmission of spiritual realities.

   d. Experienced as a mystical rite, sexual love becomes transcendental!

2. Each of us is destined, in time and through many

life-times, to fulfill our Higher Self — which is a true
fragment of the Divine Mind. "And God created
Man in His own Image, in the Image of God created
He him: male and female created He Them."

Genesis 1:27

a. That which you love in your partner is the
essential good, the Divinity, your glimpse of
his or her Higher Self that is the "true reality"
of that person.

b. Because that Higher Self you see in your partner
is a true fragment of the Divine Mind, *it is* worthy
of your devotion and worship.

c. When the time comes for the Higher Self to fully
"fill" the person, all of the lower self is caught up
into the splendor and glory of the Higher Self.
Thus, it is the total person — body and soul as
well as spirit — that is worthy of your worship.

3. All the techniques previously described are necessary
preparations for this program of mutual worship of
the Divinity that is within each.

a. The use of the psychic energizers will give the
experience of shared and enhanced vitality, and
build the energy reserves needed to attain the
higher levels of consciousness.

b. The giving and receiving of erotic massage will
develop deep feelings of trust and caring.

c. The fantasy-games and the mutual love-making
will deepen the perception of the essential good

in each partner, and will help each see the other in playing a role outside the mundane personality.

d. All these activities will draw the partners together physically, emotionally, and mentally in preparation for this next step — with the deeper levels of consciousness awakened and ready to respond to the dynamic of Cosmic Awareness.

4. Cosmic Awareness Intercourse is a true form of worship. It awakens the different levels of consciousness within the devotees and raises their love to the highest spiritual objective. *The Divine Flame fills your entire being.*

a. For each partner, the other is the chief manifestation of deity in his or her life.

b. To see Divinity in your partner likewise enhances your ability to accept Divinity within yourself.

c. The realization of the Divine Presence within is the essence of worship.

"One should worship a Divinity by becoming oneself a Divinity. One who has not become a Divinity should not worship a Divinity. Anyone worshipping a Divinity without becoming a Divinity will not reap the fruits of that worship."

The Gandharva Tantra

8

Cosmic Awareness Intercourse

Initiation ceremonies, when properly conducted and received, are like the controlled and intensified conditions to which animate and inanimate material can be exposed in a laboratory. The purpose of an initiation ceremony is to ensure that a certain effect is produced in a person by applying the necessary causes in a concentrated and often symbolic form, instead of leaving it to the changes and chances of a lifetime — or of many lifetimes — which would sooner or later produce the same developments.

Hence every initiation can only be modeled, under whatever symbolism, upon the essentials of an experience which could be undergone by the candidate in the natural course of life.

LIFE ITSELF IS THE PRIMAL INITIATOR.

And, of the rites through which Life itself can pass us, none is more potent, or more faithful in its reflection and transmission of spiritual realities, than is the experience of sexual love.

IN THE SHARED EXPERIENCE OF SEXUAL LOVE, MAN AND WOMAN MAKE THE WAY OF INNER EVOLUTION EASIER FOR EACH OTHER.

When you love a person, you tend to "idealize" that person. For very young or inexperienced lovers this can cause real problems, if they can't accept any distinction between that ideal which they inwardly perceive and the ordinary personality of their beloved. With more experience and understanding, however, you can establish the real relationship between the two.

Your own Anima image or Animus image, your personal "picture" of the ideal woman or ideal man, will undoubtedly have influenced your choice of a partner; but you can't reasonably go on measuring your partner by that standard. *But, as you get to know your partner better, you will catch glimpses of his or her best and highest self, the man or the woman your partner is destined to become.* That is the true REALITY of your partner, the person you really love.

To talk, as people sometimes do, of loving a person for his or her faults, is a confusion. Because we haven't yet met that person without those faults, it may be difficult to imagine what the effect would be; but in fact, if we love, what we love is always the BEST that's there.

Certainly, one can think one's in love with a person who merely fascinates, obsesses, infatuates. In such a case it can really be some imperfection which causes the obsession, just as sometimes we can't help running the tongue over a broken tooth, or staring at a stain on the wall. And when the object of our attention is a person, almost any attention-catcher can beglamor us. Hence the fascination of a dimple or a "beauty spot" drawing the gaze to the curve of cheek or neck. So also with a lisp, or a trick of pushing the hair back; or even, for some people, an occasional flash of dishonesty or cruelty.

Such fascinations only become love however if something is found within for love to build on. Then what one loves is the essential good, not the imperfections on the surface no matter how tolerantly one accepts these.

Again, what attracts may be a really good quality, even if for some reason it appears as a fault.

A warm, generous nature isn't a fault, even though its possessor may make errors by following it to excess. Courage isn't a fault, though a courageous person may do foolhardy or inconsiderate things. A keen sense of justice isn't a fault, even though its possessor may have real faults of intolerance or impatience.

The sunshine is truly beautiful upon the lake here and now, even though it will be more beautiful still when someone has cleared out all the junk that's been thrown in!

So, while you may perceive clearly whatever faults your partner may have, you should be able to see and love, with passionate devotion, his or her Higher Self, the person he or she is destined to become *entirely*, the perfect self which already, in reality, *is there all the time*.

THAT PERSON — YOUR PARTNER'S HIGHER SELF — IS A TRUE FRAGMENT OF THE DIVINE MIND, A PART OF THE SUPERNAL LIGHT, WHICH YOU CAN (AND SHOULD) WORSHIP IN YOU PARTNER.

THE SAME IS TRUE OF YOUR PARTNER'S PER-CEPTION OF YOUR HIGHER SELF.

Such a mutual act is *true worship;* not "idolatry" of bodies or lower natures by themselves, but a wor-ship of complete persons in their perfection.

When the time comes for a person's Higher Self to take over, it is not just a Higher Self within an "unworthy" lower vehicle. All of the person's mind and body, soul and emotions, are caught up into the Higher Self's splendor: *one person.* So when you and your partner perform the kind of worship which is now to be described — *Cosmic Awareness Intercourse* — you include your own and each other's bodies and emo-tions in the action.

WHEN YOUR ATTENTION IS FOCUSED UPON THE HIGHER SELF, YOU ARE MAKING LOVE TO A SACRED PERSON, A DIVINE PERSON, BODY, SOUL AND SPIRIT.

Both partners need to be ready for this celebration: prepared by the frequent experience of shared and enhanced vitality in the psychic energizers, by the repeated alternation of confiding trust and generous care in receiving and giving erotic massage, by the deep discovery of each in the soul of each which blossoms from mutual love-making and from the fantasy-adventures of games and play situations. They need to be so drawn together in these ways, so physically, emotionally and mentally united, that their readiness for this Cosmic Awareness Intercourse is unquestionable, is a necessary next step.

Cosmic Awareness Intercourse

A small altar, draped with a white cloth, should be set up in the place chosen to be the temple of love. A single lamp or candle should burn thereon. Flowers may be placed upon the altar as representing the natural world, and, if desired, a burning stick of incense may also be added.

1. Standing hand in hand before their altar, the lovers contemplate the lamp, meanwhile turning their thoughts in silent aspiration to all that it represents. It is token of the undying flame of Supernal Love, and of the single flame of love's ardor in which they two would burn as one.

2. Each now visualizes, centered in his or her own forehead, an intensely luminous concentration of white

light. The light is to be conceived of as so brilliant that it encompasses the whole head in a radiant glory.

When this formulation is established, the man says: I PLACE MYSELF WITHIN THE LIGHT OF THE SUPERNAL FATHER: the woman says, I PLACE MYSELF WITHIN THE LIGHT OF THE SUPERNAL MOTHER. Then both together say, WE PLACE OURSELVES WITHIN THE THE SUPERNAL LIGHT.

The visualization is allowed to fade from their consciousness.

3.   Unlinking hands and turning face to face, the partners now make adoration of one another, whether by the form which follows or by any other which they may prefer. Each section of the adoration, (A) through (E) in turn, is performed first by one partner, the man or the woman at choice; the other partner repeats it, and they continue in the same order throughout.

(A)   IN THE NAME AND POWER OF LOVE I GAZE UPON THEE, MY LOVER.

THOU ARE ALL BEAUTY; AND WITH A KISS I APPROACH THE SHRINE OF LOVE.

(A kiss is here given.)

SWEET ARE THY LIPS, MY LOVER, AND THY BREATH IS THE INCENSE OF LOVE.

(B)   THINE EYES SHINE WITH MYSTIC LIGHT, MY LOVER. I LOOK DEEPLY INTO THEM, ENHANCING THEIR FIRE WITH THE FLAME OF MY PASSION.

(C)   WE ARE ONE LIFE, ONE BREATH, ONE DESIRE,

MY LOVER: ONE OFFERING UPON LOVE'S ALTAR. IN TOKEN WHEREOF I PLACE MY HAND UPON THY HEART.

(The right hand is momently placed upon the other's heart.)

(D) THY BODY IS ALL DELIGHT, MY LOVER: IT IS THE PERFECT VEHICLE OF A CHANGELESS SPLENDOR.

(The speaker here kneels)

SO DO I KNEEL AT THY FEET, MY LOVER, IN ADOR-ATION OF THAT INMOST LOVE WHICH IS NOT THOU NOR I BUT DEITY.

(Speaker, still kneeling, performs the Charging Breath upon the partner's insteps, then upon the geni-tals; then, standing, performs it upon the heart, the throat, the brow and the crown of the head, in the last instance cradling the partner's head in both hands and bringing it slightly forward.)

(E) SO DO I LOVE THEE ENTIRE, MY LOVER: AND I GIVE THEE LOVE'S GREETING.

(A kiss is here given.)

4. The partners perform the Central Column Energizer, as given in Chapter 2.

5. After the parners have fulfilled the above pre-liminaries, they may proceed to whatever foreplay they will. Nothing is to be hurried. Only when their joy in each other has carried them to the gates of supreme desire should they proceed to the sexual union itself.

(The procedure ensuing is concerned with four factors: breathing, sexual action, visualization *and*

intention. *The visualization is moderately difficult, but will amply repay patience and perseverance; it is effective in bringing through a response from the deeper levels of the psyche, and thus helps powerfully in assuring for each partner a full participation in this Cosmic Awareness Intercourse.*

Of the Centers of Activity, three only are employed in this visualization: *

Crown Center, *representing spiritual consciousness, the Divine Presence within.*

Feet Center, *representing sensory consciousness and contact with forces of the natural world.*

Heart Center, *representing personal consciousness. This is the great transforming, reconciling and regenerating center, mediating between the spiritual and earthly natures.*

As in the Central Column Energizer, each of these centers is here conceived of as being shared between the partners.)

6.   For their union they choose a face-to-face position; either partner may be above, or both may lie on their sides, so that they can lie straight, with maximum bodily contact.

---

* The use of these centers is a traditional Qabalistic psycho-spiritual device; its purpose is always to induce a potent equilibrium of the higher and lower forces within the astral energy-system of the psyche. The energy which is built up is stabilized at the Heart Center: it is imbued with an autonomous dynamism, and is utilized in various magical techniques as a transmuting agent. In the present instance it provides an energy-source whose impetus will assist in raising the love between the partners to its highest spiritual objective.

(a) The man makes complete entry.

Neither partner makes a further movement until both have established a steady, regular and unhurried breathing, in and out together.

(b) *On an in-breath,* the man partially withdraws. In this posture, both partners visualize a single sphere of brilliant white light a little beyond the top of their heads. This visualization having been established, they join mouth to mouth in a brief kiss. (They do not kiss again until they enter upon the culminating phase of the intercourse.)

(c) *On the next out-breath,* the partners move together in a thrust, meanwhile strengthening their visualization of the sphere beyond their heads.

(From this point onwards, thrusting and drawing apart are timed to coincide exactly with breathing out and breathing in respectively.)

(d) On the next in-breath they draw apart, and at the same time visualize a darting flash of white light from the Crown Center passing rapidly down between their bodies to just beyond their feet, where it forms another sphere of white light. *(The two spheres are kept in visualization, but the flash of light is allowed to fade swiftly from consciousness.)*

(e) *On the next out-breath,* they move together in a thrust, at the same time visualizing a flash of white light passing from the Feet Center to the mid-region of the chest and forming there a third sphere of light. *(All three centers are now to be maintained clearly in visualization, but the flash of light is allowed to fade swiftly from consciousness.)*

Sections (d) and (e) are repeated throughout this first part of the intercourse while physical pleasure mounts. Steady breathing is continued, with thrusting and drawing apart co-ordinated to it. The three centers are maintained strongly in the visual imagination, the flashes of light being allowed to fade after their passing.

From time to time the partners may wish to pause: because they are practicing ejaculation control, for instance, or to introduce short intervals of simple relaxation which will in any case intensify and elevate the subsequent orgasm. When an intermission in thrusting is required, *on an in-breath* the man partially withdraws, and pauses. *The partners should, however, during cessation of physical action, continue the steady breathing and the co-ordinated flashing of light between the centers.*

Thrusting is begun again on an out-breath.

(f)   The partners continue as outlined above until, urged by an overpowering inevitability, they enter the *final* orgasmic phase of the work.

(g)   At a prearranged signal between them, the man

partially withdraws and pauses. They maintain the three centers strongly in visualization, but the passing of the flashing light is no longer visualized and their breathing is now released from its strict rhythm.

The partners join mouth to mouth in a kiss which will remain unbroken until this ritual is completed.

(h) Lying thus, they mentally formulate the intention that by their love-making, and by this holy kiss, they will reach towards, and adore, the divine in each other. *(This intention, once clearly formulated, should not be dwelt upon during that which follows; it should, however, remain in the background of awareness, where it may be calmly acknowledged and savored.)*

(i) The act of love is now re-commenced, but this time as it may carry the partners; freely, without imposition of rule or measure.

This time, when thrusting begins, two streams of white light are visualized: one flowing continuously from Crown Center to Heart Center, the other flowing continuously from Feet Center to Heart. The partners should not only visualize these currents but should "feel" them likewise in their vibrant energic flow.

(j) As desire increases the pace and intensity of

action, the Heart Center, which is the receptacle of these two currents, becomes suffused with a new light, yellow like sunshine. The partners should visualize it as becoming progressively brighter and more radiant. At last, as the climax nears, it is a furnace of intense golden light ahd heat: one heart and center of their being, one crucible in which cosmic and earthly unite and merge and blaze forth in the splendor of love's reality.

(k) When their love has been consummated, the partners remain embraced. They cease the kiss. They cease to visualize the two streams of light flowing to the Heart Center, and they allow the Heart center and the Crown Center to fade slowly from consciousness.

The brilliant sphere of the Heart Center itself remains, of the size originally visualized; but now it emits a yellow radiance which expands to envelop the partners completely in a glowing, caressing ovoid of light. For as long as they wish, they remain thus; then they allow the Heart Center, and the ovoid of extended light, to fade gradually from consciousness.

An important factor in this ritual is the long and passionate kiss which the couple share in the final phase. On at least some occasions when this Cosmic Awareness Intercourse is carried out, one or both of the partners should experience a lifting into another state of consciousness: the mystical kiss, in the conditions given, providing for some an additional aid in attaining a high rapture, a true *samadhi* (to borrow a term from India.)

Something has been said earlier (page 64) about the mystical significance of the kiss, and the sensation that it "sucks forth the soul". Initially this is a very deep and sacred Qabalistic tradition. It is said of certain holy persons that they did not "die"; when the time came for them to leave the body, the Divine Lover drew forth their soul with a kiss. This mystical doctrine, seldom mentioned, might have rested in reverent obscurity but for a youthful and enthusiastic scholar in the fifteenth century. Having devoted himself to the study of the Qabalah, Pico della Mirandola discovered this tradition, and soon incorporated it into his poems and commentaries, with emphasis on parallels in the experience of human love.

Likewise on the subject of the kiss as a profound mystical experience, the Zohar has a comment upon the beginning of the Song of Solomon:

Let him kiss me with the kisses of his mouth; for thy love is better than wine. (Song of Solomon, chapter 1, verse 2). Says the commentary:

For when mouth is joined with mouth to kiss, fire issues from the strength of affection, accompanied by radiance of the countenance, by rejoicing on both sides and by gladsome union. "For thy love is better than wine" . . . than the wine which exhilarates and brightens the countenance . . . not the wine that intoxicates, induces rage, beclouds the countenance and inflames the eyes . . . (Zohar I, 70 b.)

This passage makes it clear that earthly wine is not referred to. What the author, or authors, of the Zohar did not need to explain in detail is that wine is understood in mystical writings of whatever faith, in the Middle and Near East, as a symbol for spiritual enlightenment, an intimation of Godhead. (See Fitz-Gerald's "Rubaiyyat of Omar Khayyam"; also The Magical Philosophy Vol. IV, pages 83 through 85, and the translation of the *Terdjih Bend* of Ahmed Hatif of Isfahan which is given as an appendix in The Magical Philosophy Vol. V.)

All of which high teaching lies behind (as a singular example) the sequence of ideas which is joyfully and romantically indicated in a still well-known English song of the late 16th century:

> *Drink to me only with thine eyes*
> *And I will pledge with mine;*
> *Or leave a kiss within the cup*
> *And I'll not ask for wine.*
> *The thirst which from the soul doth rise*
> *Doth ask a drink divine —*

> *But, might I of Jove's nectar sip,*
> *I would not change for thine!*

In the last lines the poet, like a true devotee of the Cult of Love, declares he would forego direct mystical experience, preferring the divine kiss of his personal Beloved.

Cosmic Awareness Intercourse should by no means be considered a once-only adventure. The couple should renew their practice of it as often as they feel they are really prepared for it.

So true it is that those who are proficient in ejaculation control will gain most from this ritual, that Cosmic Awareness Intercourse is likely to prove a powerful encouragement to people who are learning that skill of love, to persevere and to become proficient as soon as possible. For others, the heightened experience to be gained by only brief periods of relaxation and by an unhurried progress, may in itself be a revelation. But this is only one part of a new vista of possibilities opening up for the couple through the methods of this ritual; of which more is to follow in Chapter 9.

Checkpoint
8

- Sexual love is an *initiation,* an experience which can reflect spiritual realities and transmit them to the lovers.

- Love can make you aware of the higher self in your partner, and this is a reality which is worthy of worship: not as an isolated "Divine Flame" but as manifesting through your partner's whole being.

- You and your partner are going to prepare for an act of worship of the Divine in each other! Perform your psychic energizers and erotic massage with loving confidence and tenderness; play your fantasy games so that each partner sees the other as being outside the mundane personality.

- Make a study of the directions for Cosmic Awareness Intercourse during this preparatory period. Consider the sequence of actions in the ritual. Consider the four components — *breathing, sexual action, visualization* and *intention:* each of these has a definite and regulated part in the action of the rite, and their interplay needs to be understood.

- When you and your partner are fully prepared and ready, perform Cosmic Awareness Intercourse. It is an act of worship which recognizes, as the Troubadour tradition recognized, one's partner as the chief manifestation of deity in one's life.

- Cosmic Awareness Intercourse is intended to be performed only on *one single night*, before return to your other practices and a new period of preparation for performing it again. However, Chapter 9 gives other applications of this rite, in which it is employed for longer periods.

Study Points
9

1. The practices described thus far will enable you to transcend the habit of identifying your partner with his or her everyday external appearance and personality.

   a. In addition, Cosmic Awareness Intercourse will have led you to the realization of your partner as a true spiritual being.

   b. And, Sexual Love will emerge in all its real beauty and glory, freed of the ordinariness of everyday life.

2. "To see Divinity in, and through, the beloved is to experience Divinity as love."

   a. This realization will transform your entire life — your way of seeing and experiencing the world.

   b. Sexuality, polarity, magnetism and reciprocal

relationships of all kinds will now be perceived
as nature's governing forces at all levels of life and
matter,

c. Love will now be seen as a *Cosmic Neccessity!*

3. Cosmic Awareness Intercourse is a valid and very
effective key to channeling the creative power of
Divinity.

a. In Cosmic Awareness Intercourse, the partners
are united in harmony at all levels of their being.

b. Thus united in one Divine Flame, they have the
power to bring through to the solid reality of
the material plane that which they have properly
"conceived" on the higher planes.

c. For this to happen, the energy released in sexual
action must be specifically channeled for the
fulfillment of a definite desire, and the partners
must decree it in the light and power of the
Divinity within themselves.

4. Sex Magick — the channeling of the Creative Power
of Divinity through rites of Cosmic Awareness Intercourse — involves several principles:

a. Preparation — in advance of the actual rite — to
build up energy, anticipation and reciprocity by
means of psychic energizers, erotic massage,
fantasy-games and play situations.

b. For the duration of the period (usually four or
eight successive nights) for the ritual, none

of the practices of the Magick of Sex — the fantasy-game, play situations, erotic massage, nor the psychic energizers except the Central Column Energizer — are to be performed.

c. During the preparatory period, the partners should discuss and bring to complete clarity (and mutual agreement) the benefit to be achieved from performing the ritual, without — however — prescribing (except in the case of conceiving a child) the way in which the benefit will come to you.

d. Only one objective is to be sought by means of the performance of a single ritual.

e. During all the nights of the full ritual, avoid dwelling on thoughts or images of sexual pleasure except when actually engaged in the rite.

f. Visualization of the desired object is to be very specific during the rites.

g. Upon consummation of the rite, the partners must mentally formulate the intention that that which they desire shall come into reality through the power of their Divine and inner selves.

5. The Ritual of Sex Magick for the Conception of a Child:

a. To be performed on *eight* successive nights.

b. Shall be timed to fall approximately midway between two menstrual periods.

c. During the preparatory phase, think and daydream about the child to be conceived, but do not set specifics about the secondary considerations.

d. Ejaculation to take place only once each night.

6. The Ritual of Sex Magick to Achieve Material Objectives:
   a. To be performed on six or fewer successive nights — four being generally recommended.
   b. Secure a symbol of the object desired.
   c. No ejaculation is to take place during the duration of the full ritual.

7. Sex Magick through Cosmic Awareness Intercourse takes effect by bringing into action the beneficent forces of the universe. There is abundance to supply the needs of all.
   a. "The higher the level from which the chain of causality is set in motion, the more powerful and lasting will be the effects."
   b. The actual accomplishment of the objective desired will take place along the "line of least resistance."
   c. A further natural effect of the performance of these rites is the health of the total person, resulting from the giving forth and renewal of vitality throughout the psyche and body.
   d. The outpouring of the Divine Radiance will permeate yourselves and all who come in contact with you.

9
Sexual Creativity

You and your partner will have kept up the use of the psychic energizers and of the Erotic Massage. Fantasy games and play situations, besides, will have given both of you insight into, and participation in, different facets of each other's nature, thus enhancing your spiritual unity and your ability to co-operate with one another at all levels. *Additionally, and of most vital significance for what now follows, this insight and participation will have gently and progressively detached your (and your partner's) awareness from any habit of identifying each other merely with everyday external appearance or superficial personality traits.*

MOST RADICALLY, TOO, THIS CHANGE IN THE FOCUS OF AWARENESS WILL HAVE BEEN CONFIRMED BY YOUR RECURRENT PRACTICE OF COSMIC AWARENESS INTERCOURSE.

Newer and more radiant dimensions of love, and
the realization of one's partner as a spiritual being,
are the first-fruits of Cosmic Awareness Intercourse.
For this rite is essentially a work of sexual mysticism; and those who practice it frequently, and in
full preparedness, entirely to that end will find through
it a vista of profound and continually developing,
luminous insight. To see Divinity in, and through,
the beloved is to experience Divinity as love: a personal inward realization which can but overflow to
transform the experiencer's vision of the whole of life.
Sexuality, polarity, magnetism and reciprocal relationships of all kinds will be perceived as governing
forces through all levels of life and matter, and love
itself will be seen as a cosmic necessity; which is the
cumulative verdict of Plato's *Symposium* and the
note on which Dante closes his *Paradiso*.

Some may fear a possibility that by frequent
identification of the partner with the Divine Lover,
some warm human love for the partner may be lost; but
the evidence is all to the contrary. The true face of
sexual love is not disguised by these rites: rather, it
emerges in all its real beauty, passion and devotion,
stripped of the ugly mask which the haste and pettiness
of everyday life so often fasten upon it.

Additionally to its mystical aspect, however, the
rite of Cosmic Awareness Intercourse, based as it is
on the fundamental principles of creativity, can be

utilized as a powerful instrument of sex magick. Cosmic creativity, the Western Mystery Tradition tells us, is not limited to that material level at which its effects become apparent to us: it brings the irresistible creative force of Godhead through the levels of being to the material world, which is thus fully attuned to respond to the creative impulse. In Cosmic Awareness Intercourse, the partners, united in one Divine Flame, bring into harmony all levels of their being; their love thus becoming a channel of manifestation for the creative will of Divinity Within.

Thus they have, through their performance of Cosmic Awareness Intercourse as a magical rite, the power to bring to solid reality in the material world that which they have pre-determined as the result of their action. Here we move from the Magick of Sex to a consideration of practical works of Sex Magick.

1 — Conception

The conception of a child, considered as an act of Sex Magick, is the highest, most natural and logical form of that art. In determining and bringing about the result, the partners unite to produce, in the material world, a living expression of their love and their power, an indivisible token of their oneness.

The conception of a child through Cosmic Awareness Intercourse, when both parents are practiced and proficient in that rite, is a spiritual act of special welcome for that child, creating at once an ambience of supreme blessing, of equlibrium and of harmonious good at every level for the person who comes into incarnation in these conditions.

The rite itself, with the changes in procedure noted below, will, in contradistinction from its use as in the preceding chapter, be performed upon eight successive nights. It should here be a main consideration in choosing a time for this series of eight nights, that it should fall approximately midway between two menstrual periods of the woman.

Just as for the simple use of Cosmic Awareness Intercourse, the partners should prepare themselves by means of psychic energizers, erotic massage, fantasy-games and play situations: thus they will build up *energy, anticipation* and *reciprocity.* The preparation needs to be thorough, and sufficient time should be given to it.

While the partners are bringing themselves to readiness for this use of the rite, certain general considerations apply:

(a) During the preparatory period, the partners will take a natural pleasure in letting their minds dwell on the child they hope to conceive in the rite. They can, and should, think and daydream about the child in their individual minds; they can and should talk about the child together. Both before and after birth, this child will be a product of their love for each other and also of their love for it. The partners should imagine, and should talk to each other about, the love and happiness they will be able to give the child, as well as the love and happiness which will fill their lives from the child's coming.

Naturally, too, the partners will discuss — as prospective parents usually do — whether the child will be a boy or a girl, what special joys they will be able to share with the child in this case or that, a name for a boy or for a girl. They may specualate as to whether the child will have certain tastes or aptitudes, or will inherit the looks, the voice or the talents of one relative or another. General material preparations to welcome the child are also a good thing; all this fond planning and dwelling on ideas will help get the message through to the unconscious minds of the partners, that a loved and desired new member of the family is to be hoped for and expected.

(b) *What the partners should not do* is to be "absolute" or too exclusive about secondary considerations: to fantasize about the desired child is helpful, but not to "set their hearts upon" the child being of a certain sex, temperament or inclination. That caution applies to parenthood generally; but still less should this couple, as magical partners, formulate any aspiration to bring into incarnation any specific being, or type of being. They can rest assured that their sincere preparations, and their purpose of uniting themselves at the highest spiritual level, will be met by the incarnation of one who corresponds to those preparations and that union.

(c)   At the same time, the partners should also keep in mind their purpose to give the child the great benefits and welcome of conception during the intended rites. Until that time they should be making themselves as ready as possible; any methods of contraception, therefore, which they have been using should be carefully continued right up to the commencement of the dedicated eight days.

It is also important as well as natural that during the preparatory time, the partners should take a distinctive and enhanced delight in their own sexuality, which is going to be the means of their child's bodily life. When they are together or when they think of each other at any time, it should be with an increased dwelling-upon of attraction and pleasure. A different counsel will be given for the eight days of the rite itself; but now the inclination of the partners to enjoy their imaginings of shared sexual pleasure should be encouraged to the full.

When the cycle of the rite itself is undertaken, the following considerations will apply:

(a)   During the eight nights of the rite, and the day preceding each night, both partners should so occupy themselves as *to avoid dwelling on thoughts or images of sexual pleasure except when actually engaged in the rite.*

If daydreaming about sexual pleasure were indulged in, or if during this eight days the partners shared any degree of love-making outside the ritual, it could draw away energy and incentive from the magical work and might also detract from the partners' recognition of the Divine Lover in each other.

(b) During the period dedicated to the ritual, a vivid imagining and thinking about the desired child is a good thing at any time: *excepting that during the ritual itself, this imagining and thinking is limited to specific visualizations of which more will be said presently, in the directions for the conduct of the ritual.* At other times, the partners may think, visualize, or talk together of the child in any way which will make more real to them the child's coming as a joyful fact which *is already,* on the non-material levels, accomplished.

(c) Ejaculation should take place *once each night.* Ejaculation control, or simple postponement of ejaculation by means of periods of relaxation, should be practiced until entry into the final orgasmic stage of the rite, in order to build up the intensity and magical energy of the work.

(d) For the duration of the period of the ritual — that is to say, for each of the eight nights and the day preceding each night — none of the special practices of the Magick of Sex are to be employed: not the fantasy games, nor play situations, nor erotic massage, nor the psychic energizers *except as the Central Column Energizer is incorporated into the procedure of Cosmic Awareness Intercourse.*

When the last night of the ritual is over, however, all practices may be re-commenced as the couple
normally use them.

(e)   The practice of the rite is not to be prolonged beyond the eight days and nights. The eight days
indicated for this rite represent an optimum period
for the work of sex magick under consideration: the
number eight signifies renewal, regeneration, new birth,
and magical experience shows it to be an ideal time
for bringing the forces involved to their fullness.

Should it prove that conception has not taken
place, the couple should wait until they have again
sufficiently prepared themselves, then set themselves
another eight days for the rite, as before.

For the magical act of conception, on each of the
eight nights the rite of Cosmic Awareness Intercourse
will be conducted as outlined in the previous chapter,
with, however, the following changes in procedure:

(i)   Section 2 of the rite of Cosmic Awareness
Intercourse, given in the preceding chapter, is here
to read:

**2.   Each now visualizes, centered in his or her own
forehead, an intensely luminous concentration of white
light. The light is to be conceived of as so brilliant
that it encompasses the whole head in a radiant glory.**

**Maintaining this visualization, they then visualize
above and between them a sphere of unutterable brilliance, in the center of which is seen a child in the fetal**

position.

When this formulation is established, the man says:

I INVOKE THE LIGHT OF THE SUPERNAL FATHER FOR THE ACT OF CREATION: HIS SEED IS POTENT! The woman says: I INVOKE THE LIGHT OF THE SUPERNAL MOTHER FOR THE ACT OF CREATION: HER WOMB IS FRUITFUL! Then both together say: WE INVOKE THE CREATIVE POWERS OF THE UNIVERSE, IN WHOSE GIVING AND RECEIVING THE FORCES OF LIFE ARE MULTIPLIED.

The visualizations are allowed to fade from their consciousness.

(ii) Sections 6(g) *and* (h) *of the ritual are here to read:*

(g) At a prearranged signal between them, the man partially withdraws and pauses. They maintain the three centers strongly in visualization, but the passing of the flashing light is no longer visualized and their breathing is now released from its strict rhythm. At this point they visualize a child in the fetal position, clear and luminous, within the sphere of their shared Crown Center.

The partners join mouth to mouth in a kiss which will remain unbroken until this ritual is completed; and as they meet in this kiss, they visualize the luminous image of the child descend, still in the fetal position, into their shared Heart Center. After a few moments, they allow this image of the child to fade, but retain awareness of the three centers as before.

(h)   Lying thus, they mentally formulate the intention to conceive a child in the light and blessing of their divine and higher selves. *(This intention, once clearly formulated, should not be dwelt upon during that which follows: it should, however, remain in the background of awareness, where it may be calmly acknowledged and savored.)*

2 — Achieving Material Objectives

The rite of Cosmic Awareness Intercourse can be used magically to implement many purposes besides the conception of a child: nor is this manifold use as arbitrary as might seem at first view. The forces of sex, in one aspect so uniquely specialized, have (as has been indicated) affinities with the forces of magnetism and polarity, balance and reciprocity, through all levels of life and matter; even as procreation alone can hardly be supposed to satisfy the capabilities of the fertile imagination and the teeming emotions of the endlessly yearning and aspiring, planning and exploring human psyche.

Magical sexuality permits of the fulfillment of hopes, desires and aspirations of all kinds. For this to occur, however, there are two requirements. The energy released in the sex act needs to be specially channeled for fulfillment of a definite desire; and the partners have to decree it, not in their mundane personalities but in the light and power of Divinity within themselves.

The ritual of Cosmic Awareness Intercourse provides an excellent means of meeting these requirements. We will now go on to the procedure as applied to the achievement of objectives in the material world.

While the partners are bringing themselves to readiness for the use of this rite, certain general considerations will apply:

(a) During the preparatory period the partners should discuss together, and bring to complete clarity, what benefit they hope to gain from performing the rite in this particular instance. They need to know (1) exactly what they want and (2) what change they anticipate it will effect in their lives. They should be as definite as possible on these points. Vagueness is ineffectual; while seeking too much at one time implies either mistrust of the source of supply, or expectation of some sort of haggling.

It is a good thing for the partners to enjoy constructive conversation about the happiness they will gain from the good in question; however, when they have a great deal of emotional involvement with this topic, such conversations sometimes foster negative reactions of doubt or fear as to the outcome. In such cases, each of the partners should help the situation with individual meditations, however brief; and this provides an excellent manner in which they can turn their minds to their shared purpose when they are away from each other.

The partners should understand that this type of working takes effect by bringing into action the beneficent forces of the universe. *There is abundance to supply the needs of all:* this is a literal fact. It is also a fact that circumstances on the material level can be most potently directed from the non-material levels of being, *and the higher the level from which the chain of causality is set in motion, the more powerful and lasting will be the effects.* (That is why Cosmic Awareness Intercourse provides a vital basis for sex magick.)

Magick, however, does not usually work through miracles. A "miracle" is, by definition, something which *looks* abnormal (no matter how natural its operation may be when deeply understood) and therefore a miracle causes a sense of astonishment, of shock. Those things can happen, but the more usual way in which any kind of magick works is with an appearance of complete naturalness: an invisible pressure is exerted which finds the "line of least resistance" in the earthly circumstances, and acts along that line.

For instance, suppose you and your partner perform a rite of magick — in the present context, of sex magick — for an automobile. Chances are you *won't* wake up one morning to find it sitting on your front lawn with a note from an anonymous donor. More likely, (1) someone will ask you to do some special piece of work which puts "x" extra dollars in your bank account, and (2) someone else will tell you they want to sell their automobile and you can have it for "x" dollars. (Probably the precise amount.) There are of course endless variations on this theme, but anyone with magical experience will recognize the pattern.

What is needed therefore is that you should know exactly what you want and why you want it, *but should avoid prescribing, planning or even trying to guess* HOW it is to come to you.

Discussion of the objective of the intended rite ought not to be allowed to encroach upon the special practices of the preparatory period. With regard to psychic energizers and erotic massage, it's obvious that no discussion of *anything* ought to take place while you are attending to those. With regard to fantasy games, the situation is less simple: this type of discussion ought not to take place during fantasy sessions if it is inappropriate, but in the framework of certain fantasies it may be altogether appropriate and ought, therefore, to be allowed.

For instance, a couple seriously building up for themselves a romantic eighteenth-century setting may decide to perform the rite for the purpose of acquiring a harpsichord; and this instrument will certainly have much greater emotional appeal and necessity to them as their "eighteenth-century selves" than to them in their twentieth-century manifestation. Or again, a couple may want to acquire a site where they can build a cabin for "primitive" week-ends, and this will undoubtedly mean much more — a home, in fact — to their "primitive selves" than to their "civilized selves" who don't directly relate to it. (Although the civilized selves would be well advised to look after the business details of the transaction.)

Equally, however, it would be inappropriate to expect people who are for the time being engrossed in primitive living — or in eighteenth-century living, for that matter — to consider performing a rite to acquire a microwave oven, or a video cassette recorder, which might be of high importance to their twentieth-century counterparts.

(b)   Only ONE objective is to be sought by means of this rite on a given occasion. It can be a fairly complex objective, but not overly compendious: it has to keep sufficient vividness and lucidity to engage the unconscious levels of the mind. By far the best plan is to look forward to performing a succession of rites for new purposes at reasonably-spaced intervals. Then in each case you and your partner will be able to decide constructively what is the next step in which sex magick can best help you.

(c)   *While sufficient peparation is essential,* this consideration should not become a hindrance. The great requirements are *energy, anticipation, recipro-*

city. Provided the partners are already proficient in the simple form of Cosmic Awareness Intercourse, it is far better for them to set a lot of energy circulating with, say, several weeks of specially enthusiastic use of erotic massage, psychic energizers, fantasy games and play situations, then to swing into the rite on the crest of a wave, rather than spend twelve months in careful soul-searching preparation and maybe have everything lose impetus and fall flat.

(d) For use during the preparatory period the partners should acquire some fairly small article which will *represent* the objective they are seeking to gain: e.g., a key or a tile for a house; for a car, the badge or emblem — on a key-ring, perhaps — of the particular kind of car they have in mind; if they want a horse, a suitable piece of harness such as a bit or a stirrup; if a garden, then a trowel; and so on. This symbol should be treasured by them and kept close to them, so both of them can look at it and handle it during their conversations and reflections upon the objective, and so they can see it and look at it at other times as a silent reminder of their purpose.

(e) The number of nights which should be dedicated to performing the rite for a material objective should not exceed six. Four is a number generally to be recommended, as being Qabalistically associated with the forces of prosperity, liberality and abundance: while working the rite through an over-long period could create a mood of constraint entirely at variance with those forces.

The partners may begin the series as soon as they consider themselves sufficiently prepared, and when they feel the time to be right.

When the cycle of the rite itself is undertaken, the following considerations will apply:

(a) During all the nights of the rite, and the day preceding each night, both partners should so occupy themselves as *to avoid dwelling on thoughts or images of sexual pleasure except when actually engaged in the rite.*

The reasons are as given for this same direction in the procedure for the conception of a child.

(b) During the period dedicated to the rite, vivid imagining and thinking about the thing desired is good at any time; *except that during the ritual itself, this action is to be limited to specific visualizations, of which more will be said presently in the directions for the conduct of the ritual.* At other times the partners may think, or talk together, of that which they desire; they should not need, now, to make more distinct for themselves their objective in itself, but they should be sure to realize fully **THAT TO GAIN THIS OBJECTIVE REPRESENTS A TRUE LANDMARK IN THE ATTAINMENT OF THEIR WILL, AND THAT IT WILL BRING THEM A REAL INCREASE IN EFFECTUAL LIVING.**

(Without such certainty, they could hardly find justification for performing this rite at all.)

They should also be glad in the certainty that what they desire *is already,* on the non-material levels of being, brought about.

(c) Cosmic Awareness Intercourse to achieve a material objective is to take place *without ejaculation* on every night of the rite.

This restriction is absolute, and is necessary to create a sufficient stress in the invisible levels of being, so as to carry through to material manifestation a purpose which cannot be fulfilled through the bodies of the partners. (This restriction does not apply, obviously, to the conception rite or to simple Cosmic Awareness Intercourse.)*

(d) For the duration of the period of the ritual — that is to say, for each night and the day preceding each night — none of the special practices of the Magick of Sex are to be employed: not the fantasy games, nor play situations, nor erotic massage, nor the psychic energizers *except as the Central Column Energizer is incorporated into the procedure of Cosmic Awareness Intercourse.* After the conclusion of the last night of the rite, the special practices may be re-commenced as the partners normally use them.

(e) Just as the partners should begin the rite in the confidence that that which they desire is already

---

*There is another formula of sex magick in which highly trained and practiced magicians can perform the working for any desired objective and incidentally conceive a child at the same time. This Practical Guide is not written for people who bring that much training and experience to the working; and besides, we have preferred to give a conception ritual which employs the whole power of the working to the benefit of the child.

fulfilled on the non-material levels of being, so they should complete what they have undertaken even if before its term the fulfillment of their desire has been manifested in the material world. Thus, if the partners have dedicated, for example, four nights to the ritual, and that which they desire come to pass after the first night, they should still in good magical practice and prudence complete the four nights, so as to be true to their higher selves.

(f)   If, however, the desired outcome does not follow within such a period after the working as the partners consider it reasonable to allow, they may perform the rite again for the same objective as soon as they feel themselves to be sufficiently prepared for it. At any repetition, all the above considerations will again be applicable.

For the magical act of achieving a material objective, on each of the dedicated nights the rite of Cosmic Awareness Intercourse will be conducted as outlined in the previous chapter; with, however, the following changes in procedure:

(i)   The article which has been used as a symbol of the objective should be added to the altar arrangement, and should remain there through the whole period dedicated to the rite.

(ii)   Section 2 of the rite of Cosmic Awareness Intercourse, given in the preceding chapter, is here to read:

2.   Each now visualizes, centered in his or her own forehead, an intensely luminous concentration of white light. The light is to be conceived of as so brilliant that it encompasses the whole head in a radiant glory. Each now visualizes in this light that which they desire, or the symbol of it. (For example, if the rite is being performed for opportunity to learn a certain language, this cannot easily be visualized; but a book in that language may have been used as the symbol, and that can be visualized *with understanding of what is meant by it.*) The visualization can seem like an image in front of the forehead and some distance from it, but illuminated by the light from the brow; or it can seem to be contained within the concentration of light itself. Each person may visualize in whichever manner he or she feels to be more natural.

When this formulation is established, the man says: I INVOKE WITHIN ME AND ABOUT ME THE LIGHT OF THE SUPERNAL FATHER, THAT AS I WILL, SO IN HIS DYNAMIC POWER SHALL I CREATE. The woman says: I INVOKE WITHIN ME AND ABOUT ME THE LIGHT OF THE SUPERNAL MOTHER, THAT AS I WILL, SO IN HER ALL-FORMING POWER SHALL I CREATE. Then both say: WE INVOKE WITHIN US AND ABOUT US THE SUPERNAL LIGHT, THAT AS WE WILL, SO SHALL WE CREATE: UNITING DYNAMISM AND FORMATION TO WIN ATTANMENT OF . . . .

(Here they name what they desire, in a word or brief phrase previously agreed upon by them.)

The visualization is then allowed to fade from their consciousness.

(iii) At the conclusion of Section 3 of the rite (the adoration), and before proceeding to Section 4, each partner in turn is to make the following affirmation, or any form thereof which may be preferred:

THY LOVE IS TO ME A CROWN OF LIGHT:* IN OUR UNION SHALL BE A FORCE TO MOVE THE STARS OF OUR DESTINY.

(iv) Sections 6(g) and (h) of the ritual are here to read:

(g) At a prearranged signal between them, the man partially withdraws and pauses. They maintain the three centers strongly in visualization, but the passing of the flashing light is no longer visualized and their breathing is now released from its strict rhythm. At this point they visualize that which they desire, or the symbol of it, clear and luminous within the sphere of their shared Heart Center.

The partners join mouth to mouth in a kiss which will remain unbroken until this

---

* This is so; each of the partners seeing his or her higher self in the beloved.

ritual is completed. After a few moments they allow the image of the objective to fade; but they retain awareness of the three Centers as before.

(h) Lying thus, they mentally formulate the intention that that which they desire (the objective of the rite) shall come to reality in the material world, through the power of their divine and inner selves. *(This intention, once clearly formulated, should not be dwelt upon during that which follows; it should, however, remain in the background of awareness, where it may be calmly acknowledged and savored.)*

LOVE AND WHOLENESS

The simple mystical form of Cosmic Awareness Intercourse, and the two magical forms which are given in this chapter, all bring their own specific benefits according to the use for which they are intended. In addition however there is another great good, which will come to you and your partner as a natural result of the practice of this rite in whichever form.

You will find the wonderful health of the total person, which comes from the giving forth and renewal of vitality throughout psyche and body; a strong and joyous inner activity stimulated by the love-evoked radiance of the higher self. You will find WHOLE-NESS: integration within the psyche of each, harmony

between psyche and body in each, and the wholeness of
that unity which is made up of man and woman together.

Nor will it only be you and your partner who will
benefit by this; for that outpouring of divine radiance, permeating yourselves and your relationship, has
power to strengthen, in body or in soul, all who come
in contact with you.

Checkpoint
9

- Cosmic Awareness Intercourse as given in Chapter 8 is a wonderful mystical experience. It's also an excellent preparation for sex magick. You will understand the forces you are directing.

- To perform *the conception of a child as a magical rite* is a high work of blessing and welcome for the child.

- Besides keeping up your other practices, if you are planning on performing the conception rite take note of the "general considerations" given here for the preparatory period.

- Study the considerations for the cycle of the rite, and the adjustments to the words, *well in advance* to ensure smooth working.

- For the *rite for achieving material objectives,* you and your partner need to determine *one definite goal for one cycle of the rite.* You need (a) to put it in clear-cut terms and (b) to see it as needful for a vital change in your lives.

- Prepare well, but don't over-prepare! Working for this type of objective needs freshness and impetus, and you and your partner can go into it whenever you feel you are ready.

- Don't forget *the symbol of what you desire.* Make much of it during the preparatory period and put it on your altar for the rite itself.

- Just as for the conception rite, study the considerations, and the adjustments to the words, *well in advance* for smooth working.

- Love is an essential condition for true wholeness — integration — *health* — because it is an alignment with the light and power of the higher self, whether within the individual or in the interrelationship of the couple. Remember too, *it doesn't stop at that!* Through such a person, and such a couple, the divine radiance which permeates them has power to reach others.

Appendix

Sexuality and the Tree of Life

The wonders and delights of sexual love are at every point linked with the Invisible Worlds.

This is a reality which could be set forth in many ways, but in no way more completely than according to the Western Mystery Tradition: that is, following the patterns and the teaching of the Qabalistic Tree of Life. The entire scope of human belief, aspiration, thought and action is encompassed by the sublime plan and meaning of the Tree; but basic to the comprehension of the Tree are the concepts of balance and reciprocity, of impregnation and reproduction, of affinity, attraction and harmony, which express themselves in human life chiefly in terms of sexual love.

The relationship of sexuality to the Tree of Life is fundamental to its whole concept. The history of Qabalah and of the Tree, with their sources, is long, complex and in parts obscure; but those who devoted themselves to it during the centuries in which the Tree grew to its definitive formulation, were thereby attempting reverently to interpret, in some measure, the Mind of the Creator of the visible and invisible worlds. Of the indicators available to them as to the working of that Mind, a main one was the mysterious text,

And God created man in His own image, in the image of God created He him: male and female created He them.(Genesis 1:27).

Sexuality is thus seen to be essential to the divine likeness; but, be that as it may, the resulting systematization of human perceptions of reality remains, at every level, a masterpiece.

The Tree of Life is represented by a diagram (given opposite) showing ten spheres arranged in a certain pattern and order. These spheres — the Sephiroth, to give them their Hebrew name — are connected by twenty-two Paths which also have a certain pattern and order. The esotericist needs an intimate knowledge of the Paths also, but here only the Sephiroth themselves need concern us.

Each Sephirah, or sphere, can be considered as a certain "aspect of being." BEING in its most immense and primal sense is God; and, in fact, these ten "aspects of being" are held to be initially ten distinct functions or attributes of Godhead. As such, they make up the "World" of Godhead-in-extension, the highest state of

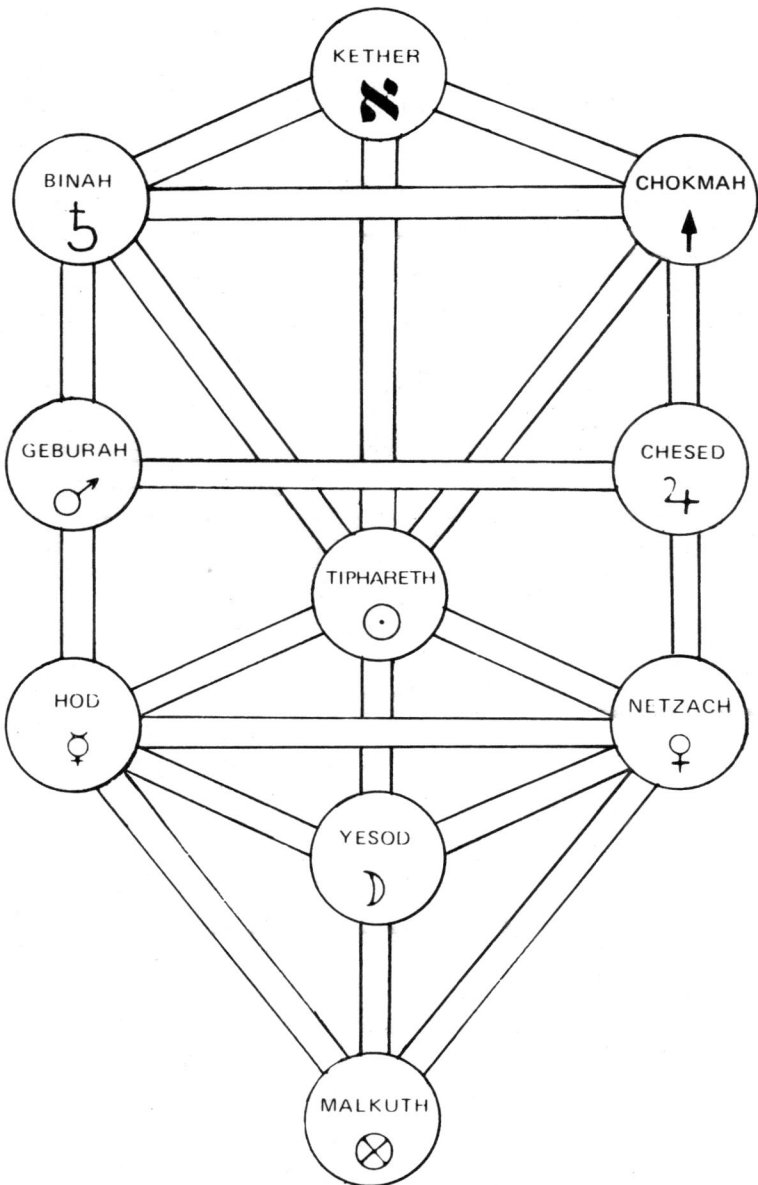

THE TREE OF LIFE

being of which humanity can in any positive way have awareness.

From that Divine "World" the Ten send forth their creative influences to form the mental, astral and material "Worlds", or *levels* of being. Thus in each "World", according to its particular mental, astral or material manner, all the ten Sephiroth exist and manifest themselves.

Despite the differences in interpretation of the Sephiroth according to the level of being which we may be considering, each Sephirah still has its own intrinsic significance which, throughout, preserves its distinctive identity; it has, also, its unchanging relationship to the other Sephiroth. In essence, what we are looking at here is not a pattern of *things* so much as a pattern of relationships, in which the "things" or concepts take their appropriate places.

The ten Sephiroth are conceived of as emanating, or "overflowing," one from another, in the downward or outward course of a mighty superabundance of energy: energy divine and infinitely creative, but initially unconditioned. The nature of each new Sephirah is determined not only by the preceding one from whose plenitude it takes its origin, but also by whatever part of the sequence is at that event already in being. In consequence, the later — the "lower" — Sephiroth are progressively more conditioned and complex in their nature than are the earlier and "higher" ones.

Thus we have the Primal Unity, Kether, which represents that from which all else proceeds. The second Sephirah, Chokmah, represents the formless and entirely dynamic impulse of creativity which can be interpreted as the very principle of maleness, or the "Supernal Father"; although illimitably transcending any concept of *personal* fatherhood which we may have.

Next in order of emanation is the third Sephirah, Binah: the Form-Giver, the Supernal Mother, who transscends all concepts of *personal* motherhood and who has as one of her symbols the primal Ocean, itself boundless and formless but source of all life-forms.

Kether, Chokmah and Binah are the three Supernals, beyond life and experience as it is generally known; although Binah has a lesser aspect which is symbolized by the planet Saturn, with the principal astrological connotations of that attribution. Here is found inspiration whether prophetic or artistic, creativity *in form*, the forces of limitation and constriction, birth and rebirth, all those ideas whose fulfillment is to be clothed in earthly matter.

Below the Supernals, but still emanating from them and in manifold ways influenced by their ceaselessly outpoured influences, are the Sephiroth whose manifestations are more directly perceived in human life. They comprise, with Saturn, the traditional planetary forces which are well known from their astrological and mythological associations; although those associations are only partial interpretations of the Sephiroth, and the full significances of the Spheres as distinct from the planetary forces go much deeper. There is also upon the Tree the Sephirah Malkuth, corresponding to the planet Earth which is not astrologically considered.

Emanating from Binah is Chesed, the Sphere of Jupiter. Although limited to certain specific attributes, this Sephirah indicates a reaction from the constrictive spirit of Binah; it is in some aspects the representative of the Supernal Father, beneath whose influence it is located on the Tree. Chesed represents the qualities of mercy, magnanimity, generosity, majesty.

This Sephirah in turn gives origin to, and is balanced by, Geburah, the Sphere of Mars. Geburah represents such qualities as justice, courage, fortitude, thus to some extent reflecting and raying forth the inflexible severity of Binah.

The Sephirah which is emanated by Geburah, however, creates an equilibrium between the forces of mercy and of justice, indeed it is the great mediating Sphere of the whole Tree: Tiphareth, the Sphere of the Sun.

Of the connotations of the Sun-sphere, something is indicated in the section headed *Morning and Night* on pages 125 and 126 of this book. From its position on the Tree, this glorious Sephirah not only resolves and unifies the forces of Chesed and Geburah: it also transmits downwards in mitigated guise the power of Kether; the power, in fact, of all the Supernals.   Thus the solar manifestation is the representative to dwellers on Earth of such high and varied qualities as impartial justice, boundless abundance, divine beauty, mystical realization and regenerative love.

A direct outpouring of Tiphareth, but coming also under the influence of Chokmah and Chesed, is Netzach, the Sphere of Venus. Here is represented the vitality and the spontaneous magnetism of the forces of nature, with love manifested as such a force, natural affection and parental devotion.

Life-giving and unconquerable though the forces of Netzach are, however, they represent in themselves only a part of the dower of Tiphareth. The Sephirah which is given forth by Netzach, therefore, is dynamically the complement of the Venus-sphere and, in its own way, is equally a development and elaboration of certain other potentialities of the Sun-sphere. This Sephirah is Hod, the Sphere of Mercury; and associated with it are such manifestations as science, medicine, law-giving and mathematics, magick and the power of prophecy.

The next Sephirah, Yesod, the Moon-sphere, reflects all the influences from above and most notably those of Tiphareth, Hod and Netzach, which in some respects modify each other. Here are represented the forces of sexuality as such, of fertility in all its forms, and of growth and increase together with the non-material proliferating, reflecting and refracting powers of the domain of dreams and of divination.

Finally, receiving the influences of the whole Tree, we have the Sephirah Malkuth, represented by this planet upon which we live and by all the conditions of material existence. Of the veiled and potential splendor of Malkuth there is much which could be added, for there is a profound affinity between the Earth-sphere and Binah.

For one thing, here on earth is the complete fulfillment of that process of materialization, that bringing to birth of spiritual force into form, which is begun in Binah. Again, the affinity between the two is comparable to that existing between a musical note and its counterpart an octave higher; and there is a sense in which Malkuth, "the Bride," is said to "sit upon the throne" of Binah, the Supernal Mother. So far is the venerable tradition which we are considering, from seeing anything essentially "shameful" or unworthy of reverence in the wonderful material world, and in the implications of our existence herein. It is, however, the turning-point in our journey; here is completed our *involution* into material life, here begins our *evolution* of spiritual development.

The relationship of Chokmah and Binah, Supernal Father and Supernal Mother, is the primal manifestation of sexuality in the patterns of the Tree of Life. This relationship represents a sublimity beyond any human manifestation of sexuality, but yet, reflected in many dimensions, it becomes the prototype of every sexual

relationship.

Further down upon the Tree, it is Hod and Netzach, the recipients of varied influences and complex currents of force, which become the most characteristic representatives of Man and Woman as they are known in the world. This attribution is supported by a text of the Zohar which states that children are "the fruit of the Two Willows" (Zohar IV 169b) — "the Two Willows" being, by tradition, one of the titles in which Hod and Netzach are linked together.

At a more inward level, however, there is a potent polarity between Netzach, the Venus sphere, and Geburah the Mars sphere:* the irresistible power and tide of natural life appearing sometimes as an implacable destiny, while the courage and severity of Geburah produce a deep spirit of alliance and of warm fellowship.

Some of the vertical relationships of the Tree also find significant echoes in human thought and belief. The relationship of Sun to Earth is in some mythologies interpreted as sexual; in others, that of Moon to Earth or of Sun to Moon. Likewise, since every Sephirah is conceived of as being "female" in its relationship to the one from which it is emanated, and "male" in relation to the one which emanates from it, every one of the Sephiroth except Kether and Malkuth can

---

* Those who know the Paths will recall that the influence of Mars reappears even upon that Path which links Netzach with Hod.

on that score be validly considered as representing either sex; while Kether, as origin of all, and Malkuth as receptacle of all, must equally have at least the potential of both sexes within them.

It is, furthermore, entirely in keeping with Qabalistic thought to consider all the Supernals, in some circumstances, as a single unity; hence we may hold those mythologies also to be represented which feature either a Sky-father and an Earth-mother as progenitors, or, more anciently, a Sky-mother and an Earth-father. All these configurations have their place in the human imagination, springing from the deep and often, otherwise, unrecognized life of the psyche.

For the Ten Sephiroth, besides being shown forth in the four levels of the universe as a whole — the Cosmos — are also reflected in the spiritual, mental, emotional-instinctual and physical nature of each human being — the Microcosm. The cosmic Tree of Life represents, inevitably, distinctively human conceptions of Godhead and of the universe; the microcosmic, "inner" Tree represents with most illuminated insight the inner nature of each individual.

Each person, whether man or woman, reflects in his or her individual nature (the psyche with its many components, and the physical body) the complete Tree of Life; some of its parts may be represented in more developed form than others in this or that person, but in each the whole Tree, represented by the corresponding attributes of the individual nature, must, ultimately, be realized and integrated.

With regard to the Earth-sphere which, in this context, represents the physical body and simple sensory consciousness, no further explanation is needed; nor with regard to the "planetary" Sephiroth whose well-known astrological attributes all have their place, albeit in evidence to a greater or lesser extent, in every human psyche.* The case of the Supernals, however, is here particularly interesting.

Binah has, as in the cosmic Tree, a double attribution: that of the Sphere of Saturn and, here, of the Anima (corresponding to the Supernal Mother.) Sometimes, as in the Qabalistic "Dark Mother", in the image of "the Shulamite," in such perceptions as Durer's "Melancholia" and in the Jungian "Dark Anima", the Supernal and Saturnian identities of Binah are merged; but that is not invariably so.

Chokmah is represented in the psyche by the Animus, corresponding to the Supernal Father; while Kether is represented by our "personal Kether," that "bud of light" or "nucleus" in the Divine Mind which is both the "Idea" which is the individual's origin, and the "Star" or Divine Flame" to whose unity we must eventually, perfected, attain.

---

* " . . . the psyche is not a unity but a 'constellation', consisting of other luminaries besides the sun. . . . These lesser lights are, on the old view, identical with the planetary correspondences in the psyche which were postulated by astrology." — C.G. Jung, *Mysterium Coniunctionis*, pp 357-358 (Bollingen Foundation, N.Y., 1963.)

This is the Supernal Triad as it represents the divine nature within to the developed perception; or, in the interim, as it is experienced through our myriad perceptions of its reflected rays.

Our spiritual progress can be represented in two ways, and there is no contradiction between them. The way which comes nearer to human experience of the matter is to regard it as a progress *inwards*, to deeper and deeper levels of being. The way in which it is more easily described in detail, or represented diagrammatically, is to regard it as a progress *upwards* on the Tree as it is traditionally figured.

It is, then, by thus progressing through the successive levels of our own nature, that we are able to ascend to the spiritual heights.

THAT IS THE ONLY WAY OF ASCENT WHICH IS OPEN TO US, WHETHER WE MAKE THAT ASCENT IN A MOMENT'S ILLUMINATION OR IN THE COURSE OF LIFETIMES.

It is possible to take such a purely mystical account of the inner development of the individual as that given in Chapters XIX and XX of *The Dark Night of the Soul* by St. John of the Cross, and without any great subtlety of interpretation to show how the ten steps of the "ladder of love" there described follow the attributes of the ten Sephiroth, beginning with the soul's turning from worldly things on the first step (Malkuth) and ending with the soul's "complete assimilation to God" on the tenth step (Kether): a description which is the more impressive because its author is in no wise concerned to follow any formal plan, but only to record his sincere perception of that progress. Our subject, however, is to relate the Tree, not to solitary mystical progress, but to sexual love.

The way is the same; but in sexual love the aids are great. The plan of the whole Tree of Life is set for each person to integrate inwardly through life's experiences; but the Tree represents life in its entirety, both in its male and its female aspects. It follows, therefore, that Man will find some of its lessons harder to learn, while Woman will have difficulty with others.

If, however, the man and the woman unite their powers, finding through sexual love the ability to create a united identity and thus to make each other's life-experience their own, then together they have the key to every mystery. They can go forward, invincible in their love.

Thus the way of sexual love is as privileged as that of the dedicated mystic. Says the Zohar, that dark but abundant mine of Qabalistic tradition,

For there are two lamps: and when the light of the one on high is extinguished, by the smoke that issues from the one below it is re-lit. (Zohar I 70b.)*

That is: although in your life the Sun-sphere of mystical realization may not have been disclosed to you by spiritual means, yet the "smoke", the misty

---

* All quotations from the Zohar in this book are from *The Zohar*, tr. by H. Sperling & M. Simon (Soncino Press, London, 1933.)

astral light of sexual love in the Moon-sphere, may be the means whereby it becomes illuminated, making mystical realization resplendent for you.

Be it so for all true lovers!

Glossary

ANIMA The supreme female principle as present to the unconscious levels of the psyche; not directly accessible to the conscious mind, and not part of the personality.

ANIMUS The supreme male principle as present to the unconscious levels of the psyche; not directly accessible to the conscious mind, and not part of the personality.

ARCHETYPAL IMAGE The form in which an *archetype* is clothed by a particular culture, mythology, religion or individual. Thus, while *Anima* and *Animus* are archetypes and formless, we all have in the depths of the psyche known or unknown 'images' associated with them; the Anima image influencing man's idea of woman, the Animus image influencing woman's idea of man.

ARCHETYPE A universal and imageless concept; here, in the sense used by C. G. Jung, such a concept existing within the collective unconscious mind of humanity.

ASTRAL Pertaining to that level of existence which is finer and more penetrating than matter, but denser than mind. In the psyche, it comprises the emotional/instinctual levels which unite mind and body.

CENTERS OF ACTI- -VITY Energy-centers of the astral body, corresponding to neural or glandular centers in the physi - cal body: the "chakras."

EMOTION A state of consciousness arising from the promptings of one or more *instincts,* or from some higher impulse which may have become correlated to the instincts.

EROTIC Apt to arouse sexual desire.

EVOLUTION Progression from a low and confused state to one of development and specialization; here, the ascent of our nature towards its spiritual goal after its *involution* (descent.) *(Qabalistic doctrine.)*

FANTASY A "waking dream", either involuntary or (as here) deliberately planned and aided with appropriate clothes and other articles.

FOREPLAY Sexually stimulating and enjoyable actions shared by the partners before intercourse.

HIGHER SELF That part of the psyche which is more elevated than the rational mind: the Higher Unconscious, the Spirit.

INSTINCT An innate, sub-rational and usually unconscious impulse, prompting living beings to act in given ways in certain situations which are critical to them.

INTEGRATION The organization of parts into a united and harmonious whole: e.g., of a man and a woman into a united couple, *or* of the various components into a united personality.

INVOLUTION Descent from a simple and primal ideal or from a high development; here, the descent of our primal spiritual being into the earthly condition. *(Qabalistic doctrine.)*

LOWER SELF The soul and the physical body together: the rational, emotional, instinctual, lower unconscious and material levels of human nature.

LUMBAR REGION The part of the back below the lowest ribs.

MATURATION The act or process of becoming mature, fully developed: of a human being, this is understood to mean coming to mental and emotional besides bodily maturity.

PENILE Relating to the penis, the male organ of sexual intercourse.

PERINEUM The muscular

bridge between the back of the sex organs (in man or woman) and the anus.

PRESSURE POINT Any of a number of points on the body where a nerve which controls a specific sensation (e.g., hunger, pain in a given area, anxiety, sexual desire) passes sufficiently near the surface to react to finger-pressure. Such pressure-points are sometimes far from the site which is affected by their use.

PSYCHE The non-material part of a psycho-physical being.

PSYCHIC Here used in its first sense, of "relating to the psyche".

QABALAH A venerable Wisdom Tradition which was formulated chiefly in Mediterranean regions; Hebrew and Greek are its principal languages.

RELAXATION The loosening of tension; especially a systematic and progressive loosening of tension in the voluntary muscles throughout the body. During sexual intercourse, for both partners from time to time to relax the tensions caused by mounting excitment is a way to prolong and intensify pleasure.

SEPHIRAH (plural form **SEPHIROTH**) One of the ten 'Voices from Nothing' or aspects of being which are represented as ten spheres or circles upon the Qabalistic *Tree of Life* (see below.) Their names, with literal meanings, are as follows:

Kether, Crown;*Chokmah,* Wisdom; *Binah,* Understanding; *Chesed,* Mercy, *Geburah,* Strength; *Tiphareth,* Beauty; *Netzach,* Victory; *Hod,* Splendor, *Yesod,* Foundation; and *Malkuth,* Kingdom.

TREE OF LIFE *(Qabalistic)* A traditional glyph representing the Ten Sephiroth (see above), the "aspects of being" which are perceptible to mankind as existing both in the outer universe and in the psyche. They are depicted as spheres or circles arranged in a certain way to show their equilibrium, and are interconnected by twenty-two paths.

TROUBADOUR One of a class of poets and composer-singers of certain Mediterranean regions, who in the 11th, 12th and 13th centuries produced numerous lyrics on themes of love, thereby considerably influencing subsequent western literature.

VISUALIZE To form a mental image. The important factor for success in this is the knowledge that the image is to be mental, not an optical illusion. It can however *seem* optically visible in some cases.

Also by Melita Denning and Osborne Phillips

THE LEWELLYN PRACTICAL GUIDE TO
PSYCHIC SELF-DEFENSE & WELL-BEING

> *FACT: Every person in our modern world is sub-
> jected, constantly, to psychic stress and psycho-
> logical bombardment: advertising and sales pro-
> motions that play upon primitive emotions, polit-
> ical and religious appeals that work on feelings
> of guilt and insecurity, noise, threats of violence
> and war, news of crime and disaster, etc.*
> *FACT: Each person (and every living thing) is
> surrounded by an electro-magnetic Force Field, or
> AURA, that can provide the means to Psychic
> Self-Defense and dynamic Well-Being.*

This book explores the world of "psychic warefare:"
showing the nature of genuine psychic attacks, the
reality of psychic stress, the structure of the psyche
and its inter-relationship with the physical body. It
shows how each person must develop his weakened
aura into a powerful defense shield—thereby gaining
both psychic defense and dynamic well-being that can
even extend into protection against physical violence,
accidents . . . even ill-health. And it gives exact instruc-
tions for the fortification of the aura, specific rituals
for protection, and the Rite of the First Kathisma
using the PSALMS to invoke Divine Blessing.

*FACT: This book will change your life! Your developed
aura brings you strength, confidence, poise, the dynamics for success, communion with your Spiritual Source.*

250 pages, "put-you-in-the-picture" illustrations, powerful techniques for individual and group use.
ISBN 0-87542-190-3, soft cover.   US $6.95

If not readily available from your book dealer, send
full price, plus $1.00 postage & handling, and 5% sales
tax if Minnesota resident, to Llewellyn Publications,
P.O. Box 43383-MS, St. Paul, MN 55164-0383, U.S.A.

Also by Melita Denning and Osborne Phillips

THE LLEWELLYN PRACTICAL GUIDE TO
THE DEVELOPMENT OF PSYCHIC POWERS

*You already have the ability to use ESP, Astral Vision,
Divination, Prophecy, Dowsing, Mental Telepathy! You
simply have to know how to exercise and develop your
abilities.*

Written by two of the most knowledgable experts in the
world of magick today, this book is a complete course,
teaching you, step by step, how to develop powers that
have always been yours since birth! Using the techniques
they teach, you will soon be able to move objects at a
distance, see into the future, know the thoughts and
feelings of another person, find lost objects, water and
even people using your own latent talents.

Psychic powers are as much a natural ability as any other
talent. You'll learn to play with those new skills, work
with groups of friends to accomplish things you never
would have believed possible. The text shows you the
tools you need, the exercises you can do—many any
time, anywhere—and how to use your abilities to change
your life and the lives of those close to you. The pleasure
and joy you'll receive as you discover new things about
yourself will last a lifetime.

ISBN: 0-87542-191-1, 244 pages, soft cover   US $5.95

If not readily available from your book dealer, send
full price, plus $1.00 postage & handling, and 5% sales
tax if Minnesota resident, to Llewellyn Publications,
P.O. Box 43383-MS, St. Paul, MN 55164-0383, U.S.A.

Also by Melita Denning and Osborne Phillips

ROBE & RING
BOOK I OF THE MAGICAL PHILOSOPHY

> *Most men worship divinity as God absolute or as
> one of many gods and pray to such divinity for
> goodness in life. For a small number this is not
> sufficient, and they seek instead a closer bond—
> to love or be loved by their God: these are the
> mystics. Of these, a smaller number exists for
> whom even this divine love is not enough. For
> these, the magicians, to know and love their God,
> it is necessary that they should realize and bring
> into their consciousness their own divinity.*

This is the Western Magical Tradition. Its methods are
active rather than passive, and ceremonial rather than
meditative—although meditation is utilized when occasion requires. The secret of its initiatory teaching is
that it should follow the lines of development of the
psyche itself. It is Western, too, in its emphasis upon the
cultivation of the individual personality, and upon the
attainment of conscious unity and integration between
the higher self and the ordinary personality.

In this book, you will discover the glory of the Western
Tradition; here are the ethics, the ideals and aspirations
of the Initiate, the vivid imagery, the rich ceremonial,
the wonder and the wisdom of High Magick. In this
book, you understand the importance of FINDING
YOUR TRUE WILL and following it to YOUR self-
realization; you learn how to begin "growing" your
Magical Personality, and how to furnish your own
personal Chamber of the Art.
ISBN 0-87542-176-8, 192 pages, hardbound   US $10.00

If not readily available from your book dealer, send
full price, plus $1.00 postage & handling, and 5% sales
tax if Minnesota resident, to Llewellyn Publications,
P.O. Box 43383-MS, St. Paul, MN 55164-0383, U.S.A.

Also by Melita Denning and Osborne Phillips

THE APPAREL OF HIGH MAGICK
BOOK II OF THE MAGICAL PHILOSOPHY

> *The power of ritual to make contact with the hidden levels of the mind is very subtle, and yet very simple. No matter how deeply the subconscious mind may be buried beneath inhibitions, rationalizations or, frequently, beneath loads of ephemeral rubbish, one line of communication must remain open: that is through the sympathetic nervous system upon which we all depend to look after our digestion and our breathing, and even to keep our heart beating while we sleep.*

This book shows you the how and why of many forms of traditional symbolism, the "apparel" in which the Magician clothes his inner purposes so as to make an IRRESISTIBLE RITE for their fulfillment in the material world. It is with such symbolism that we catch the attention of more than the rational mind, reaching all levels of consciousness and welding them into a single instrument of power.

In this one book you will find the symbolism of minerals, gems and amulets; occult significance of metals, use of talismans, stones and colors; symbolism of the calendar, magical seasons of the year; mathematical views of the universe; plants and their occult significance; animal archetypes; the primary correspondences of ceremonial magick and the Qabalah; magical equipment and exoteric symbolism of the elemental weapons; the Tarot; the holy and mysterious mansions of the Moon; Exercises and techniques of Meditation.
SIBN 0-87542-177-6, hardbound   US $10.00

If not readily available from your book dealer, send full price, plus $1.00 postage & handling, and 5% sales tax if Minnesota resident, to Llewellyn Publications, P.O. Box 43383-MS, St. Paul, MN 55164-0383, U.S.A.

Also by Melita Denning and Osborne Phillips

THE SWORD AND THE SERPENT
BOOK III OF THE MAGICAL PHILOSOPHY

THE MAGICK OF YOUR CHOICE. Yes, you can build an original, workable system of Ceremonial Magick, based on the authentic traditions of the Qabalah and the Ritual Keys for activation and control of the ASTRAL LIGHT.

You may not wish to use the traditional Hebrew forms, nor even the Greek or Roman forms whose correspond-ences on the Tree of Life have long since been indicated by such authorities as Aleister Crowley and Dion Fortune. YOU CAN EMPLOY WHATEVER MAY BE THE PANTHEON OF YOUR CHOICE—Celtic, AmerIndian, Haitian or other—and, by following the method set forth in this book you can construct a valid system whose Qabalistic basis none can challenge!

Contrary to the ideas which have in the past been put forward by traditional schools, Qabalah is a self-con-tained system needing neither Hebrew nor Christian dogma. Qabalah supplies the framework for any deific system—making POWER MAGICK THAT EXPRESSES YOUR WILL in perfect reciprocity with the Forces of the Cosmos.

In this book you will learn the basic Qabalistic doctrines and the full range of correspondences—*the mystical keys to consciousness.* You will learn how the channels can be contracted by the appropriate rites, how the astral substance is molded by thought, etheric forces and Movement within the Light, the Cosmic Tides, develop-mental exercises and magical techniques, etc.
ISBN 0-87542-178-4, hardbound   US $10.00

If not readily available from your book dealer, send full price, plus $1.00 postage & handling, and 5% sales tax if Minnesota resident, to Llewellyn Publications, P.O. Box 43383-MS, St. Paul, MN 55164-0383, U.S.A.

Also by Melita Denning and Osborne Phillips

THE TRIUMPH OF LIGHT
BOOK IV OF THE MAGICAL PHILOSOPHY

THE WISDOM OF THE WEST: the Western Mystery Tradition of self-development leading to that "descent of Light" crowning Man as KING—fulfilling human destiny—is based entirely on knowledge of the structure of the psyche. It is this that uniquely distinguishes the Western Way from the Eastern, and the modern from the old.

What is the true function of the Ego? How real is the psychic difference between Man and Woman? Can human love really "inspire" us? What is the reality of your "Holy Guardian Angel?" What is the Abyss? There is no "side-stepping" as these questions are answered, nor in the account of many other pertinent topics which are evaded by other authorities writing in this field.

Here, in this book, is a luminous suming-up of Western Man's adventures in self-discovery; here is a guide-book to the relationship between psychological integration and occult progress; here is the deepest and yet most lucid exposition ever made of what actually takes place in the psyche at various stages of its progress. *And, because this book embodies the principles of GNOSIS, to understand these matters IS TO UNDERGO INITIATION and to develop THE FOUNDATIONS OF PERSONAL POWER.*

The Wisdom of the West is shown to be a true path of spiritual development and mystical enlightenment and vindicated as that most suited to meet today's needs in contemporary Western culture.
ISBN 0-87542-179-2, hardbound   US $10.00

If not readily available from your book dealer, send full price, plus $1.00 postage & handling, and 5% sales tax if Minnesota resident, to Llewellyn Publications, P.O. Box 43383-MS, St. Paul, MN 55164-0383, U.S.A.

Also by Melita Denning and Osborne Phillips

VOUDOUN FIRE: THE LIVING REALITY OF
MYSTICAL RELIGION

*OBJECTIVE PROOF OF SPIRITUAL REALITY.
Spectacular full color photgraphs of actual psychic
phenomena filmed during Voodoo rituals in Haiti
give objective proof of powers and forces normally
invisible, and of the Power and the Glory that is
part of the valid religious, and magical, experience.*

In this book, you see for yourself the ASTRAL FIRE
that accompanies genuine ritual; you see the living
presence of the LOA as they are invoked; you witness
the visible possession of the devotee by a spiritual entity, and the ecstasy upon her face. 39 full color plates,
8½" x 11" page size, and many black & white photo-
graphs demonstrate the reality of psychic phenomena
and the authenticity of Voodoo as religion and system
of magick.

The text gives a concise history of Voudoun, tracing
not only its African but AmerIndian origins and its
beginnings back into ancient Egypt. Parallels with
Christianity and with pre-Christian European religions
are demonstrated, and the distorted myths which represent Voodoo as evil are shown for what they are.

The religion itself is analyzed, its dances, chants, musical
and magical instruments, its gods and rituals described.
Voudoun is made to come alive for the reader and its
music is presented in words and score set to disco beat
for personal experience.
ISBN 0-87542-816-6, 182 pages, softcover   US $9.95

If not readily available from your book dealer, send
full price, plus $1.00 postage & handling, and 5% sales
tax if Minnesota resident, to Llewellyn Publications,
P.O. Box 43383-MS, St. Paul, MN 55164-0383, U.S.A.

Forthcoming from Melita Denning and Osborne Phillips

THE LLEWELLYN PRACTICAL GUIDE TO PLANETARY MAGICK

> *Planetary Magick, also called "Qabalistic Sphere working," is one of the most important types of esoteric working — yet it is also one of the most jealously guarded techniques of Knowledge & Power.*

This book provides a complete cycle of workings based on the simple planetary system of the Seven Spheres — thus avoiding the complexities of Qabalistic theory while still operating within the age-proven system. Rites based on the planetary formulae open the doors to healing, meditation, exaltation of consciousness, sex magick, and spiritual integration.

While providing a comprehensive overview of the process — and giving explicit guidance in such matters as the creation of the astral environment in which the subtle forces are manipulated, the assumption of specific mental attitudes to awaken the archetypal forces and thus to truly work with power, ceremonial action that translates symbol, myth and imagery into physical action to thus liberate the flow of specific energy and to direct it for particular achievements — the book is not limited to any one system of deific forces or words of power, but will be acceptable to all. Further, the material is presented in such a way that it may be used in encounter groups, psychological processes of integration, and a multitude of New Age practices.

This technique may also be used to balance weaknesses and problem areas in one's natal horoscope, and to strengthen the influence of a planet making a favorable transit in matters of electional astrology.

To be advised of publication of this book, and to receive further information about it, write to Llewellyn Publications, P.O. Box 43383-MS, St. Paul, MN 55164-0383, USA, and ask to be placed on our mailing list.

Also by Melita Denning and Osborne Phillips

THE LLEWELLYN DEEP MIND TAPE
FOR ASTRAL PROJECTION

INDUCING THE OUT-OF-BODY EXPERIENCE
A powerful new tool combining guided Mind Pro-
gramming techniques with specially created sound
and music to evoke deep level response in the
psyche and its psychic centres for controlled
development, and projection.

This is a tool so powerful that it is offered only for use
in conjunction with *The Llewellyn Practical Guide to
Astral Projection!* Melita Denning and Osborne Phillips,
authors of the book and adepts fully experienced in all
levels of psychic development and occult training, have
designed this 90-minute cassette tape to guide the student
through full relaxation and the preparations for projection, and then — with the added dimension of personally
produced synthesizer sound patterns — to program
the deep-mind through the stages of the awakening, and
the projection of, the astral Body of Light. And then
introducing the programming to guide your safe return
to normal consciousness — enabling you to bridge the
worlds of Body, Mind and Spirit.

WHY PROJECT? Because you are an Astral as well as a
physical being — and you are intended to be a Whole
Person. Your entry into the Astral World initiates a
whole new stage in psychic and spiritual growth, and a
renewal and rebirth on the physical plane as well:
opening the way for new Health, Vitality, Success, and
expanded levels of consciousness.

Order No. 3-87542-201, 90-minute cassette tape. $9.95

If you have the book, *The Llewellyn Practical Guide to
Astral Projection,* you may order this *Deep Mind Tape* by
sending full price, plus $1.00 postage and handling, and
5% sales tax if Minnesota resident, to Llewellyn Publications, P.O. Box 43383-MS, St. Paul, MN 55164-0383 USA